SUSATO

by ALFA

SCRIPTORA

Published in Great Britain 2012

by
SCRIPTORA
25 Summerhill Road
London N15

©Erika Goulden 2012
Revised version 2013
Reprinted 2015 and 2016

This is a work of fiction, with a factual historical background.

ISBN 978-0-9562494-5-6

Printed and bound by Witley Press Ltd, Hunstanton PE36 6AD

For my family
and my Jewish neighbours
in Liverpool
and all my relatives
in Germany
with love

**For my family
and my Jewish neighbours
in Liverpool
and all my relatives
in Germany
with love**

Melodies of forgotten moments
haunt her
a place without shadows
a pale sun
the wind silent

As her heart embraces solitude
words turn into radiant colours

1

Once upon a time there lived a beautiful young woman named Irmi alone on an island among millions and millions of words.

She lived there in a sturdy wooden house surrounded by icy waters, glorious bluebells in spring, high, dancing grasses in summer, rust and white clumps of heather in autumn and gales and patchy snow in winter.

Before she left her hometown Susato she gave various excuses, lies really, to her relatives and friends, hoping to disappear without trace forever. She did not want them to know her real reasons for leaving because she was absolutely certain that they would not understand. Nobody knew about her island. It had to be her precious secret.

When the burning flames of those copper beech trees reached her heart on long, lonely walks along the medieval walls which enclose the centre of her beloved old town her desperate yearning for solitude, stronger than ever, forced her again and again to escape to her island.

Lately she longed to stay there with her words for ever, even if it meant leaving her Susato where centuries come to life in narrow, cobbled lanes with its nooks and crannies, half-timbered houses and magnificent churches, its prolific past extending as far back as Neolithic times: a Hanseatic town which played a crucial role in the structure of medieval Germany.

It had not been an easy decision to leave Susato and her relatives for ever but this powerful and painful need for solitude which had tormented her throughout her whole life, even making her feel guilty, dominated her every thought.

Now, on her magical island she hopes for solace within solitude, strengthened by her friends the words, who understand her dilemma.

Irmi's Island

2

Now begins the story of a very special family and their town which the writer Irmi wants to share with her trusted friends the words, who are already waiting patiently to welcome her on their island.

Susato is 'The secret capital of Westphalia', so they say proudly, which has been a settlement since Roman times, first mentioned in 836 AD.

Its impressive twelfth century Charter and Municipal Code served as a model for many German communities. A rich, old trading town with its agricultural and cattle market for the surrounding most fertile region, the Börde.

That is why Brana, Irmi's grandmother, a beautiful, dark-haired girl with glowing skin, simply arrives here one day from Poland in 1890 and finds work and shelter on Farmer Moller's farm. Nobody is asking why she came any more because she is such a private, yet cheerful worker. Even if they had she would not have said anything. She just smiles and walks away. Her German isn't all that fluent, her accent heavy.

"Brana, what sort of a name is that? Are you Jewish?" No answer. She is, of course.

She marries Joseph Hofer, a Catholic brought up in an orphanage, and soon has four daughters.

Joseph works for a railway company. A proud, committed socialist, highly intelligent, who tries to bring about changes for his fellow workers, better wages, working hours and conditions, the need for sickness benefit and pensions. Every month he holds meetings in his local pub, thundering from his pulpit.

Brana and Joseph with their daughters Sarah Ruth Yetta and Toba

'We have to do something lads, even strike."

Of course, many agree with his arguments but are much too afraid to lose their work.

"Let's think about it, Jupp. These are difficult times. At least we still have a job to go to. Have another Schnapps, Jupp, go on!"

Schnapps is Joseph's weakness. Quite often Brana has to send Yetta, his favourite daughter, to the pub to bring him home.

"Sorry, Yetta, but he will listen to you."

Yetta is a sickly child who adores her father and his speeches. She hates poverty as much as he does, did so all her life. Joseph is ambitious for his daughters. He does not want them to be servants for a rich farmer like his wife used to be.

"Skivvies, emptying their piss-pots," are his warning words. "Find something better, aim higher. I never had the chance. In the orphanage they didn't even give us a bit of string to keep our trousers up. Always keep your hands in your pockets, lads, they said, so we couldn't run away."

4

And yet there is a gentler, less angry side to his nature. Joseph loves music and because of his leadership qualities has become front-man of a brass band. Yetta is so proud of her handsome, tall father in his smart uniform with his well-trimmed *Kaiser Wilhelm* moustache when they march through the town and he throws his baton high up, never drops it.

Then, one day Yetta's life falls apart. She is eleven.

"Go and get your father!" Brana demands.

Yetta feels for her mother, especially when she is this upset.

Joseph is very drunk and very guilty when he sees Yetta, his always loving daughter. They walk home holding hands. It is late, getting dark.

"No, no, don't sing, father! The neighbours will hear and talk."

Joseph touches her face and goes straight upstairs to bed. There are only two small bedrooms in this tiny house which belongs to Farmer Moller, given as part of Brana's wages because she still works for him.

When Joseph is drunk or when she wants to avoid sex Brana sleeps with the girls. Only two beds for five, not very comfy. Still, this is her noiseless way of coping. She hates arguments.

Suddenly, in the middle of the night all five are woken by a scream. They rush at once into Joseph's bedroom. But he is not there. The only window is wide open, rain coming in. It is raining with real force. When they try to close the window a pitiful sound comes from the street below.

"Jupp...Jupp...father...where are you?"

The girls are crying. They find him on the pavement, bleeding. In his drunken stupor he has mistaken the low window for the door and has fallen out.

Noise and commotion have woken the neighbours. Someone brings a wooden cart. Joseph is lifted on. Brana and the girls want to get him to the hospital which is near by. Two are pulling at the front and three push at the back, all still in their night-wear, now wet through. Too late! He bleeds to death on the way.

Next morning the neighbours point to long scratch marks right down from the window. Probably made by his fingernails when he was trying to hold on somehow.

That memory is to haunt Yetta for ever and explains many of her attitudes and actions in later years.

There is no pension from the railway company for the widow with four young daughters. They might even have been glad to get rid of this rabble-rouser. Who knows?

But his workmates, who always liked and admired him, start a collection for a decent funeral.

Brana continues to work for Farmer Moller. At least they have a roof over their heads. She also takes in blood-stained washing from the abattoir. Yetta recalls with bitterness:

"Sometimes she came to bed wet through to her underwear, too tired to take those clothes off, rubbing soapy suds all night on a washboard in the kitchen."

Farmer Moller tries to help. He knows what a good worker he has in Brana, doesn't want to lose her. He likes her too. Every week she is given potatoes, cabbage, carrots, turnips, even bones to make soup. This helps to provide a basic diet for the girls, stew mainly. And on festive occasions Brana brings home a good-sized chicken.

However, unkind, perhaps even jealous, neighbours did speculate. Not to her face, of course.

"That fat farmer never helped anyone before. He is probably hoping for a little private gratitude from her. She is still a beautiful woman and with Jupp out of the way to protect her, well..."

Did she? Those who liked her thought it very unlikely.

6

Funny, but Yetta never lost her love for those very special *Sieglinde* potatoes.

"I used to fish them out of the stew, even if my sisters screamed blue murder. Never liked carrots, though."

Yetta

3

Irmi is sitting in the sunshine on her island waiting for the sky to explode with words. She enjoys watching them flying in to occupy their usual nesting places. Acid words settle comfortably next to ridicule. The wounding keep away from the healing. A single, loving word shivers alone, pushed back by a group of bitter, angry, hysterical utterances, as always. Irmi reaches for the shivering one, holds it in both hands and carries it into her house. There, a glowing wood-fire will soon help to strengthen it again.

On the table stands an open jar of black treacle next to a large knife and a loaf. Bees are enjoying the treacle.

I should have put the lid back on, but never mind... Soon the loving word stops shivering.

"Do you remember your Grandma Elizabeth, Irmi?" Of course she does. How can she ever forget her?

"Let's go and remember her then, please, please."

"And why not? Come on then!"

A familiar smell of cinnamon lures them back to a small house in Susato. The very moment you step into the house, feel your way through the dark, narrow hallway up some wooden stairs the smell is there. Even Grandma seems to smell of it.

Grandma's kitchen is more like a small living-room where every piece of furniture is far too big. Stepping through the door you find yourself in front of a large, rectangular table with a lace table-cloth. Behind the table is a sofa full of hand-embroidered cushions, all lined up. Nobody ever sits on that sofa, there isn't enough room to squeeze past the table.

Alongside the wall, close to the sofa, is Grandma's armchair. And there she sits, propped up against a big, square pillow. Her face is small. She has very blue eyes and a plait of brownish hair wrapped all around her head. Most of the time she wears a pinafore dress, darkish with a red blouse.

To her left, not more than an inch away, is a cupboard with glass doors. Lace curtains on the inside hide what is kept in there. But of course Irmi knows: cups, saucers, sugar, butter and black treacle. Another smaller cupboard carries two big, white enamel buckets filled with water from the well. But the most important pieces of furniture in this room are two visitors' chairs, heavy, wooden chairs with tall backs and soft seats. One stands close to the stove, Irmi's favourite, the other by the always open window. Grandma has many visitors. The chairs are often occupied when Irmi arrives. So, she simply returns a little later, hiding outside, waiting for the visitor to leave.

Irmi is a shy girl, never says much. Grandma understands, just smiles. Irmi likes to listen to that very special Westphalian dialect. Grandma never speaks anything else, no High German, *Hochdeutsch.*

When it is just the two of them Grandma reaches for her stick by the sofa and slowly, very slowly, forces herself up out of the armchair. One of her specially made shoes is heavy, black and bulky. She limps over to the tall cupboard, then back to the table, pushes the tablecloth aside and cuts a large slice of bread with an enormous knife. Then spreads butter and treacle on the bread and hands it to Irmi. There she sits, safe and warm, no longer troubled.

Irmi often wondered what had happened to Grandma's back but could never bring herself to ask, because that horrible girl from over the road and her brother called Grandma *Quasimodo,* pointing to the church just around the corner, shouting real loud:

"When is she going to ring the bells, your ugly Gran? Next Sunday?"

9

Once Irmi asked her mother Yetta, married to Grandma's son Heini, Irmi's father. Her embarrassed answer was:

"She fell out of her cot when she was a baby."

Anyway, it never really mattered to Irmi or her father. Yetta, well...

Looking back now, Irmi understands a little better. Had her mother been afraid that her children might inherit Grandma's deformities?

Grandma Elizabeth, a stern Protestant, is a widow like Brana. Her husband died in the First World War. She gets a widow's pension from the Army which helps her to live a modest but comfortable life. She does not have to work like Brana, who has no pension.

Her two children are son Heini and daughter Erna, who lives with her. She never married. Erna is Irmi's favourite aunt. Family members mention now and then that she is a bit, you know, backward and under Grandma's thumb.

"But we are not going to remember all that now, are we? Not today, anyway."

The loving word nods. It has gathered real strength again. Irmi returns it to a group where it might be safe now.

Grandma Elizabeth

4

In Brana's house poverty is less painful now. The girls have started work and have not forgotten their father's words:

"Aim for something better, girls!"

Ruth and Toba have apprenticeships in the largest department store in Susato, *Rosenbaum,* Ruth as a seamstress and Toba, the youngest, in the curtain department. Yetta finds work in a bookshop. The owners, an older couple, do not have children and treat her as if she was their own daughter. Yetta loves books. The customers like her enthusiasm and friendly advice. Only Sarah, the oldest, goes into service on Moller's farm which does not help her general lack of confidence. However, she has inherited her mother's love for working on the land, especially when it is harvest time.

Brana with her adult daughters

On pay days the girls give their wage-packets to Brana. They receive pocket money, not much, but are only too happy being able to help their never complaining mother.

The time for courtships and jealousies begins. The first to fall madly in love is Ruth with a well-heeled suitor. She is the most beautiful of the four girls, stunning, and she knows it, elegant in every way, her mother's pride and joy. Brana makes sure there is always enough money for her. New, more expensive clothes, which is not always fair to her sisters.

"Why doesn't she make her own clothes? She's supposed to be a seamstress, isn't she?"

The truth is Ruth hasn't the flair or interest needed to be really good at what she does. She should be sewing net-curtains for Rosenbaum's customers which is about her limit. Toba should have been the seamstress. She has natural talent and already makes all the clothes for herself, Yetta, Sarah and her mother. Real stylish too!

Toba

In the evenings they all sit in the tiny living-room which now has a sofa, their prize possession. They are working on a dowry for Ruth, embroidering tablecloths and monograms onto handkerchiefs and bed-linen. Yetta's work is the best and neatest. She enjoys it but also resents that her mother seems to do more for this daughter than for the other three.

On summer evenings the window is kept wide open when the sisters sing those lovely folk-songs. The neighbours look forward to this and listen until dark. Poor Toba always hits the wrong notes. This really annoys her sisters.

"Just forget it, Toba. You are spoiling it all." Of course, she never listens.

Susato has many impressive churches. As all the girls are brought up as Catholics, Ruth's wedding is going to be in the Romanesque Patrokli-Minster. Separated only by the width of the pedestrian area stands Sankt Petri, the oldest church in Westphalia.

These two churches in the centre of the town are protected by a medieval wall made from local sandstone. Two thirds of this wall and its dry moats have been preserved and a walk along it in early spring, when all the trees are in bloom, is a joy.

Irmi will miss this walk and its trees.

It is Ruth's wedding day. She looks stunning. Toba has created her wedding dress, a dream in cream.

"You do it, I have other things on my mind," is Ruth's excuse.

She would never admit that Toba has more talent, even without proper training.

All are waiting for the wedding cart to arrive. It is a sunny day. Suddenly, Horst, the groom's best man, comes running up the street. Knock ... knock...

"Come in, come in! What's up?"

"I have to speak to Ruth now, alone."

They go upstairs.

"Ruth, I am so sorry. Alfred has disappeared. I don't know where he is. I found his note just now, by chance really."

He hands her the note.

Horst,

I cannot marry her. Don't ask why. You will never see me again. I know you love Ruth more than I ever did. Marry her today and look after my child.

Your friend Alfred

Ruth is in shock. She walks over to the window with his note, ripping it into tiny pieces, not saying a word, forcing herself not to cry. Confused, her mind is racing.

Something very serious must have happened to him to do this. He loved me, I know he did. Maybe the baby ... or am I a complete fool? I should have suspected something was wrong. Why didn't I? Can love be that blind?

Then anger takes over completely. She throws her veil on the floor still trying not to cry.

The lying bastard! What a love performance! Only to get me to... How dare he tell Horst to marry me after he has had his fun.

What sort of a person does he think I am? A fool, Ruth, a fool, fool, fool. I hate him. No, I don't. Yes, I do. He does not deserve me or the baby.

Horst is getting more and more anxious. What is she going to do? Why doesn't she say anything? Pride? At last she stops staring out of the window and looks at him trying to think more clearly.

If Horst really does love me enough to be ridiculed like this by his best friend maybe he is right for me and the baby.

She cannot hold back her tears any longer, lies on the floor in her beautiful wedding dress, sobbing, sobbing, sobbing. Horst kneels down by her side, takes her hand and strokes her hair.

"So sorry, my beautiful love."

"Sorry for you too. He deserted both of us. You know I don't love you. Are you still willing to marry me?"

"Of course, hoped you would want that. We'll work it out together. I have always loved you, always will."

"Thank you, Horst. I will be at the church as planned. Just tell the priest. He knows me but do not tell the others downstairs. Please hurry!"

Everyone is waiting to hear what has happened, but Horst simply rushes to the door.

"Don't worry, it's nothing, only a surprise for you all. You'll see later."

It takes a while until Ruth comes down, defeated, pulling at her veil. It took all her strength to put it back on. She even manages to smile but Brana knows her daughter too well.

The wedding cart arrives. It looks lovely. The neighbours have decorated it with cornflowers and poppies, not really Ruth's favourite flowers. She would have liked something more stylish perhaps, not Farmer Moller's field flowers. But did that matter now?

Nobody talks on the way to the church. A surprise he said, yes, good or bad? They are uneasy. Horst looked much too upset. They soon find out. And what a surprise it is!

Ruth pretends to be happy, even gives Horst a long, passionate kiss at the altar. Can she really fool them all? And who knows about the baby? Brana? No, she never even told her mother.

Horst has saved her from disgrace.

Ruth

16

5

All day the words have been pestering Irmi wanting to know more about Ruth and her on-the-spot-decision to marry Horst.

"We'll come back to it some other time," she tells them, cleverly hiding her own confusion. But to keep the words happy before she goes on her evening walk to the woodland she leaves them with her own thoughts about marriage, tongue in cheek, of course, or is it?

Is it all worthwhile
I ponder with a smile
an ever growing doubt
makes many lovers shout
what is it all about?
For ever and ever
and no one else never
who thought of it first
some fool without thirst?
Or is it that fear
we wouldn't be here
in some hundred year
if lust doesn't stir
the juices within
for a kid and some kin?
So, let's celebrate the day
come what may
rain or shine
the outcome sublime
at least

SOMETIMES

"See you later, my nosy friends. Behave yourselves! Remember, you are only words after all, forever ready to comment, even criticize. I should know. Have some humility and empathise with Ruth instead."

Irmi walks slowly, very slowly towards her woodland. And there it is, her confidant, the old oak-tree, alone in the still air, softly blue. A tired wilderness has stopped breathing. Only the aspens move their leaves with a slight shiver of green and silver, stroking modestly flowering shrubs. Fresh mountain waters, clear as liquid glass, kiss wet alder bushes, secretly, in a hidden corner of the woods. Powerful tree trunks speckled with light reign over undergrowth, covered in glowing red berries, waiting in vain for the song of a bird. Dark moths open their wings once more in the narcotic, resinous scent of a spruce and tiny insects dance feverishly in much hated shade. A painful light ripples onto a last golden space of open woodland. At its edge dimmed streaks of sunlight, gruesome, milky. Dipped into blue dusk a glorious day makes room for long evening shadows. A last silent flash of light before the moon throws cold rays into the branches of a pine tree.

Irmi comes here when she is looking for solace, when guilt takes over her whole being. Why can't she be like other people? Her desperate need for solitude has always been stronger than anything else in her life, even ignoring the love for her family and Susato. She escaped early into her own world, a child, refusing to fit in, just listening and observing people around her, always looking for a way out, forever the outsider.

When she found her friends the words and now this tiny island, she knew that it was right to let solitude win. For the first time she belonged.

As an adult she learned to pretend to be part of the world her relatives and friends lived in. Not easy! Who would understand anyway?

Irmi simply had to choose solitude, prepared to pay the consequences. Still there were her usual doubts:

Is it right to be that self-indulgent? Is it natural? Shouldn't people need people? Can the words ever be enough?

How often has she asked her silent, old friend the oak-tree these same questions? As always she feels safe and protected leaning against the strong tree trunk stroking its rough bark, trying not to cry.

"I know you at least do understand. Standing here all alone, allowing me to rest and find peace under your powerful branches for a while, forever patient. Thank you so much."

It is getting really dark now. Irmi is on her way back home.

Hope the words have gone to sleep.

Irmi's Tree

6

Brana and Ruth are sitting on the sofa in the living-room. Brana is hoping that Ruth will open up and talk about herself, the baby and Horst. She doesn't.

"Could do with a sofa like this one myself. No chance."

"We'll see, dear."

Ruth knows her mother will find a way to get her that sofa.

Horst works for the Railway Company like her father used to. The wages are modest but at least he has work, not like Heini, Yetta's beau, who has been unemployed for the last four years but is hoping to start work on Hitler's *Autobahn* soon. Ruth has stopped working for the Rosenbaums because of her pregnancy. Also, Horst does not want her to work any more.

"People will think I cannot support my own wife," he says with pride.

He tries everything to win her love, spoils her. But she resents him, aware of what neighbours, even some friends are thinking, judging her. Some are counting the months of her pregnancy, gossiping about her with glee:

"She'll say the baby was born early, just you wait and see. But we know better, don't we? It serves her right. She thought it was clever catching herself that fat fish. Always wanted to be better than us. Money, money, money... She should have known that rich men don't want girls from our poverty-stricken backgrounds. Only good for one thing, of course, what else?"

In spite of all that Ruth desperately wants this child. She hopes it will look like the man who deserted her, the man she still loves and cannot forget, dark eyes and dark hair, not like Horst blonde and blue-eyed.

Brana feels sorry for Horst. He is so good to her daughter. They are waiting for Yetta, Toba and Sarah to come home from work, Horst and Heini too. Toba arrives first. She seems upset.

"What is it, Toba?"

"I'll tell you when we are all here. I'm starving."

"You are always starving."

They laugh.

Sarah comes home with a big basket full of goodies: potatoes, carrots, cabbages. Farmer Moller is making sure he is not losing his best workers.

"Thank God for Sarah!" They smile.

Toba has grabbed a carrot. Sarah loves Toba more than her other sisters, looking after her when she was only a baby and Brana had to work long hours. Food remains scarce in Brana's home in spite of Farmer Moller's help. Anyway, many people were hungry after the First World War but Sarah always made sure Toba was not, often denying herself the last piece of bread so that Toba could go to sleep not feeling hungry.

"Let's put the stew on! They'll all be starving soon." As always, Toba and Sarah enjoy cooking together.

Next to arrive is Yetta. She puts Hitler's book *Mein Kampf* on the table.

"What's that smell?"

"Sarah and Toba are making stew."

"Put plenty of spuds in, remember, only a few carrots. I hate them."

"We will, you and your potato madness."

Even today potato-stew remains Yetta's favourite food.

Heini has arrived and notices *Mein Kampf* straight away.

"Where did that come from?"

21

"Brought it from the shop. We've just had a new delivery. They are selling like hot-cakes. Every couple about to marry is expected to buy one. That's us, isn't it, Heini?"

"You didn't pay good money for it, did you?"

"No, Mrs Goldberg gave it to me. Read it carefully, she said, and let me know what you think of it."

"I hope you do."

"Why, have you read it?'

"Of course I have. Mind you, lots of his ideas to examine yet, but the main theme is racial madness, based on hatred."

"Are you all listening to our professor Heini?"

"Thanks, Yetta, but did Mrs Goldberg know that the students outside Berlin University burned books on a bonfire last weekend? Books by Jewish, Marxist, Bolshevist and other so-called *disruptive* authors like Karl Marx, Thomas Mann, Maxim Gorky and many more, even my favourite poet Heinrich Heine. Dangerous, aren't they, books, especially to the *Third Reich*. Careful, wherever they burn books, they might burn people next!"

"Don't be ridiculous, Heini! Playing the know-all, are you?"

Heini always wanted to be a teacher but his widowed mother Elizabeth could not afford to let him study on her modest war-pension. He reads a lot and is also a member of an amateur dramatics group, still free of Nazi members. But for how long?

The door opens.

"Heil Hitler!" Horst marches in, his right arm raised high.

"Hail Caesar!" is Heini's response.

They laugh, but Horst is serious. He recently joined the Nazi Party and looks after teenage boys of the Hitler Youth in Susato. He loves it. He wants to be somebody in the eyes of his wife and perhaps sees this as his chance.

"You should join, Heini. Without Hitler you would still be unemployed. What a great idea his Autobahn is!"

"No, don't," Toba interrupts, "you know what happened today at Rosenbaums. They put a sign up at the main window."

Germans retaliate! Don't buy from Jews! If you do, you are a traitor.

"And you wouldn't believe this! They even put two military looking fellas outside the main entrance of the shop to stop customers from coming in, handing out leaflets."

"What did the people do, Toba?"

"Some ignored them, but others became frightened and left."

"What about poor Mrs Rosenbaum?"

"I felt so sorry for the old woman at her till. She is nearly seventy, you know, and has always been so kind to me. Last week she asked me to make her a special dress for her seventieth birthday."

"Did you know, Toba, she offered Heini and me a flat in her big house in *Thomästrasse* when we are married?"

"Yes, I did know. Mother was so happy for you. We all know how difficult it still is to find somewhere."

"Come and get it! The stew is ready." Silence.

Somehow their family meal does not taste as good as usual. Brana is not eating at all. Too much salt perhaps?

7

Irmi is furious, running stark naked down to the sea. She simply has to cool down. Words, words, words, especially all those Hitler-words, are driving her crazy. When did they hatch and escape, let loose to do so much harm? And who backed them with action?

The sea is stormy and icy cold, stroking her, ignoring her tears. She thought she knew a lot about words. Maybe that group of bitter, angry, even hysterical utterances would understand her fury today. And what about that delegation of busy but meaningless words who always intimidate the modest, shy, lost and confused, stopping them from having a mind of their own? She has met them all.

And what about the peacemakers, Irmi's favourites, trying to intervene, sometimes helped by a colourful but unstable gathering, protecting the status quo? Another group of confident, too often influential expressions believes in transformation, but a large group of deadly words remains sceptical, backed by expert concealers.

Not forgetting the thoughtless, twittering on happily in unison with those neglected by feelings. But even more dangerous are words said and not meant or words meant and not said which have recently been trying to pollute their nesting place on Irmi's island. So far all of them were welcome as long as they didn't get out of hand like those Hitler-words.

But why fool herself, thinking words can always be controlled? She knows that they must remain free and powerful but unfortunately are too often open to exploitation.

Irmi has forgotten to bring a towel but the sun is strong enough now to dry her slowly. Suddenly, sitting on her favourite boulder, a voice interrupts her thoughts.

"Isn't it a glorious day?"

Next, someone is putting a shirt around her shoulders. Who is it? It can only be the old man who comes once a week in his boat to deliver her provisions. Irmi likes him. He never stays long, never asks questions. But that wasn't his voice. She turns round and there he stands, a young man, tall, with the most beautiful red hair. She has always admired red-heads, even envied them.

"Don't worry, I won't look. Dad is sick, so I had to come. Hope you don't mind."

"Thanks for the shirt, just take the things into the house." He smiles.

"My name is Wonderful, what's yours?"

"Fury."

"Really. Can I help in any way?"

"If you have a mind of your own I would like your reaction to some words which have upset me deeply today."

I must be desperate, she thought, *asking a complete stranger into my world.*

He is already walking ahead, giving her time to hide her nakedness under his shirt.

Waiting for her, standing awkwardly in the middle of the room he thinks:

Lovely room, cosy. Lots of books on many shelves. Mind you, she has to entertain herself somehow. Wonder what she is reading at the moment?

A book lies open on the table next to a vase of wild flowers. He looks for the title: Hitler's *Mein Kampf*

I don't believe it!

26

She returns in a long kaftan, her hair still wet. "Coffee?"

"No, thanks. Have to get back. Dad, you see..."

"Sorry, of course, didn't even ask what's wrong. Much too involved with myself and these murderous words."

"He has been vomiting all night. Tell you what, I'll come next week with plenty of time to spare if you want to talk. Okay?"

On his way out he has doubts.

This one is a funny one. No wonder she lives all alone on this island. Do I really want to come back, especially if Dad is well again next week?

Irmi is confused when he leaves, surprised how much she needed someone to talk to.

8

Sarah, the oldest and most mature of the sisters, is worried about her mother. Since the day they heard about the Rosenbaums, Brana is withdrawn and much too quiet. Even Farmer Moller noticed it. Does he know about her Jewish background? Probably guessing. These are confusing times. Not that Brana ever told anybody about herself. The neighbours think she is a Polish Catholic and that is good, especially now. Mind you, there have been sly comments from them lately.

"You never go to Mass, do you, Brana?" or

"You never got married in church, did you, Brana?"

Even within the family they only know that she ran away from a feudal Lord and Master in Poland who treated his workers like slaves.

"Can still see him now," Brana used to tell them, "sitting high up on his horse, even using a whip if we didn't work fast enough on the fields. And the pretty girls, well, they weren't safe from him, know what I mean..."

Only Brana's magical lullaby survived from that time in Poland. She used to sing it to her girls when they were very small. Even now they remember some of the Yiddish words.

Schlaf, Kindlein schlaf!   **Sleep, little one sleep!**
Dein Vater hüt' die Schaf   **Your father guards the sheep**
Deine Mutter schüttelt's Bäumelein   **Your mother shakes a tree**
da fällt herab ein Träumelein   **down falls a dream for thee**
Schlaf, Kindlein, schlaf!   **Sleep, little one sleep!**

As children they were never aware that their mother was Jewish, Polish, yes, they knew that. Brought up as Catholics they went to Mass very early every morning before school with the other children. Of course their father knew but he never mentioned it and sadly he died before Brana's secret became dangerous for his family.

Brana used to visit a woman friend secretly. Sarah overheard them speaking Yiddish once. She never told her sisters. Brana was upset for a long time when this friend died of cancer. She still goes to the cemetery *Nottebohmweg* regularly, takes pebbles to place on her grave. Again, only Sarah knows.

It is potato-harvest-time. Usually Brana's favourite time, out on the fields come rain or shine. Not too much rain, mind. At lunch time mother and daughter sit under an old oak tree waiting for Farmer Moller to bring hot *Muckefuck,* a coffee substitute made from roasted wheat, cheese and *Mettwurst,* a Westphalian sausage speciality.

"We have to talk, mother. Please don't go to the cemetery anymore. It is much too dangerous now. What if they find out about you? They'll make you wear the Yellow Star, maybe even all of us. Because you are our mother, we are supposed to be the same through you. I only found that out recently. Even children as young as six have to wear that star now."

I know, Sarah, but what can I do?"

"We have to talk it over within the family. We simply cannot continue to ignore it, not now. Just think what they did to the Rosenbaums."

"But what about Horst? He is so involved with the Hitler Youth. Even more now, so Ruth tells me."

"We'll see! Sunday is a good time when we are all together, especially when Ruth brings sweet little Clara."

Sarah

9

It has been a week now. Irmi is still trying to come to terms with all those Hitler-words which made her so furious that day when she met Wonderful for the first time. She has written some of them down in case he does come so that they can look at them together. When she dreamt about his beautiful red hair she thought:

Nothing wrong with that. I am not getting involved. And anyway, he might never come again, trying a little too hard to convince herself.

For many years now Irmi has been struggling to understand how things could have escalated as far as they did, especially the systematic murder of the Jews. Who would ever understand the horror of it and the why?

Irmi was only a young child after the war. Nobody in her family or even at school ever spoke about it, or offered some explanation, however futile. Perhaps a sense of shame, guilt, even betrayal kept many silent whilst others claimed that they didn't know what had happened in the Concentration Camps. In her teens Irmi was deeply troubled, starting to believe that there must be something evil deep down in her, being a German. She started to keep a watchful eye on herself.

Hitler's *Ideology of Racial Nationalism is* lying on her kitchen table, an accurate blueprint of what he planned to do, even though few believed at first that he intended to carry out every phase of his political philosophy.

The basic theme, based on hatred, is racial. Germans should be racially pure, superior Aryan people. Their duty should be to increase their numbers in order to fulfil their destiny of world

31

supremacy. The mixing of blood could only be corrected if the lowest elements, the Jews, were weeded out.

The black-haired Jewish boy waits for hours with satanic joy in his dark eyes for the unsuspecting Aryan girl, whom he shames with his blood and thereby robs the Nation.

He seeks to destroy the racial characteristics of the Germans with every means at his command. To tumble them from their cultural and political heights, so to raise themselves to the vacant places.

From *Mein Kampf* by Adolf Hitler

These are the words which had made Irmi so furious that she had to cool off in the sea but also curious to know how did Wonderful deal with the atrocities of the Second World War? They are both about the same age.

I'll go down to the sea, sit on my magic boulder and wait for him. It is Wednesday, my usual day for the provisions to be delivered. He might come after all.

The beauty of the island is helping to calm her emotions. More *horror words* are hiding behind a large rock, too scared to torment her further.

Under her open window, strangled by weeds, lilies of the valley. Their smell stroking her softly in sunlight of liquid amber. Her garden is still as wild as always. She likes it that way with curtains of wisteria, all around her. Crimson, unopened buds and a buddleia-tree covered in blue butterflies lift her spirits from darkness to joy. Further down by the sea the splendour of white cumulus clouds, like a dream ship heading for her Susato...

10

It is that Sunday now which Sarah suggested to be right for the talk about her mother's safety. Brana is nervous. She agrees they have to talk about it, but is worried about Horst. She likes him and understands why he is so involved with the Hitler Youth and other activities to do with the Nazi Party. Ruth has no time for him. All her love goes to the child Clara. She doesn't even want Horst to be near the little girl. Keeps her away from him whenever she can.

"She is my child, Mother, not his." It saddens Brana.

Heini and Yetta

Yetta and Heini are married now, renting two rooms downstairs in old Mrs Rosenbaum's large house in *Thomästrasse*. The old lady lives upstairs. She told Yetta the other day that her son and his family are planning to go to America, now that the Nazis have closed the department store.

"Don't tell anyone, Yetta. I am too old to go with them. Why should I anyway? Susato is my home. I love the place, lived and worked here all my life. Sorry about Toba though, losing her job in our store. You know, she stayed with me to the end, even when they smashed all the windows. Luckily she is young and such a talented girl. She'll survive. Wonder whether I'll ever wear that lovely dress she made for me for my seventieth birthday? But without my family here..."

Sarah and Toba are busy baking *Apfelkuchen*. Ruth and Clara are first to arrive.

"Oma, Oma, look... my new dress!"

She dances around the room.

Brana gives her a big hug. Her first grandchild. What a blessing, in spite of these difficult times.

Heini arrives next but without Yetta. Clara dashes to the door.

"Uncle Heini, uncle Heini, we are having apple cakes today."

"Fantastic, Clara, my favourite cakes too." Heini takes Clara's hand.

"Let's go into the kitchen. I can smell something sweet. Can you?"

" I can, I can."

She jumps up and down. Sarah and Toba are happy to see Heini. He is always so jolly.

"You two take the cakes in. We'll bring our very best *Muckefuck.*" Clara is so proud to help.

They all squash onto the sofa. Clara sits on Brana's knee.

"Where is Horst, Ruth?"

"He should be here soon. Left a week ago. Training days in a youth-hostel with his Hitler Youths at *Möhnesee,* the Möhne dam."

Now, there he is.

"Heil Hitler! So you are starting without me, are you?"

"Heil Hitler, Papa, heil Hitler!"

Clara is excited, clinging to Horst.

"Come and finish your cake, Clara!"

It is Ruth's stern voice, but Clara holds on to Papa. Sarah pours Horst a large cup of coffee.

"Why is Yetta late, Heini? She is never late. We better not start without her."

"She has terrible news for you, folks. Worried out of her mind about Brana, crying all the time."

Toba interrupts.

"I'll get the knitted doll for the child. What did you call her, Clara?"

"Schätzelein."

Toba takes Clara upstairs, removing both of them from the bad news to come.

When Yetta arrives Sarah gives her a big hug. "Come and sit here! I'll bring you a cuppa."

Yetta looks sad and worn out.

"It's about Mrs Rosenbaum. You wouldn't believe what they have done to the old woman. SA thugs marched her along *Thomästrasse* with many other Jewish folk. All wearing large, heavy placards around their necks. I couldn't read what was written on them. Lots of people were lining the street, shouting at them, real nasty, even throwing foul apples. One hit Mrs Rosenbaum in the face. I could see it all, hiding behind my net curtains in our front room, wondering what the commotion was all about. And there she was, our Mrs Rosenbaum. She could hardly walk. Why didn't I run out to help her? Why, why, why...?"

Brana is crying.

"I am glad you didn't."

"No, Mother, no. Now they have got me too. No courage to help the woman who was always good to all of us, worried only about my own safety. I feel so guilty."

Horst walks over to her, but she pushes him away.

"Where did they take them, Horst, and why? Do you know?" Horst's face is very red.

"Yes, I do know. Someone came to the youth-hostel to tell the young boys that those Jews had to be punished because they insulted the *Führer* and their Swastika flag. The boys jeered. They love their *Führer* and the flag. Hitler has given them a sense of purpose and importance."

Heini is furious, walking to the door, then comes back.

"Teaching them to hate, Horst, and brainwashing them to be racist Germans. Lies, all lies, nothing but lies."

He hands him *Mein Kampf.*

"Read it, Horst! It's all in there. Your *Führer* simply wants to get rid of all the Jews. How can you belong to such a bunch of fanatics?"

No answer from Horst. He is looking at Ruth. No reaction from her. She is getting up to leave the room.

"Wait, Ruth, what about Brana? How can we protect her now? They are bound to find out about her. You have to help, Horst, now!"

He is sweating. Of course, he wants to help. They are his family.

"Perhaps this might work. What about sending her to a fake-funeral to her sister in Dortmund or wherever. She never comes back. Very sick suddenly, unable to travel, that sort of thing."

"But what about those always nosy neighbours? Many do their *Heil Hitler* bit already. They could be dangerous."

"You are so right, Sarah. Mother still says *Good Morning.* I've warned her many times."

Even Ruth has something to say now.

"I should know about neighbours. Do they know Mother has a sister?"

"It doesn't matter, Ruth. Act, convince them! Spread the news around the neighbours anyway. It might keep Brana safe, for a short while at least."

"But where do we hide Mother instead, Horst?"

Yetta is crying again. Heini goes over to her, touches her face and gives her his dirty hankie.

"I've got an idea, Yetta, but we have to be quick. Things are escalating more and more every day. I'll tell you as soon as I know for sure, promise."

11

After that family Sunday Yetta and Heini go home early.

"You told them you had an idea how to protect our mother. How Heini? Tell me now!"

"You'll see. First, let's go and see my mother."

"Your mother? How can she possibly help?"

"She might. Anyway, it's about time we told her about our baby."

Yetta looks worried. She is trying to hide her fears from Heini. Will their baby inherit his mother's disability? She mustn't spoil it for him. He talks about *his boy* all the time, happy as a lark. It will be the first grandchild for Elizabeth.

The welcome is warm as always. Only Heini's sister Erna is not herself today, no smile.

"We've come to bring you our good news. Yetta is having a baby."

"Oh Yetta, how wonderful!"

Elizabeth tries to get out of her armchair. She stumbles. Her stick falls to the floor. Heini picks it up quickly, laughs and helps his mother up. How tiny she is, how frail! Yet her eyes sparkle and that smile, well... But Yetta only sees the cripple. *Please God, not that!* Her thoughts are racing.

Erna hasn't said one word, which is not like her. Heini goes over and gives her a big hug.

"You'll be our boy's auntie. What about that, eh?"

No answer. Erna has started to cry.

"Erna, Ernalein, what is the matter? Aren't you happy for us?"

Elizabeth knows the reason.

"Erna received a letter a few days ago. I'll show you."

It is an official looking letter. Heini reads it quickly. Erna is asked to make an appointment with two doctors regarding sterilization. Should the doctors agree then there would be a court hearing deciding whether Erna should be sterilized. Sterilization is proposed for people with mental illness, the disabled and even slow learners like Erna who went to a *Sonderschule,* a special school to help children with learning difficulties. These schools are now closed.

"And all that to keep the Aryan race pure."

Heini is fuming. He hands the letter to Yetta. His hand is shaking, standing in the middle of the room shouting.

"First the Jews and now my sister. I can't believe what that bastard is getting away with. Now even doctors and the law are on his side."

Erna is a tall, big-boned woman, blonde, with a broad face and a body like a feather cushion, gentle, kind. Made to be a mother, in its old-fashioned sense that is, warm, patient and lots of fun. She looks after her neighbour's children now and then. The kids love her. She is engaged to Franz, a soldier, who is stationed in Berlin at the moment. Erna has stopped crying.

"How can I tell Franz? We wanted to get married in the summer and have children, naturally. What can I do, Heini?"

Elizabeth is sitting in her armchair again, looking even frailer. In her heart she blames herself for Erna's situation. They are judging her because of me is foremost in her mind.

Heini has calmed down for his sister's sake.

"Don't tell Franz just yet. Ignore the letter for a while. Wait and see what happens. Someone might shoot Hitler in the meantime. I'll see what I can find out for you. Horst might know."

Yetta is touching Erna's face, stroking her hair whilst her own worries are close to hysteria.

39

"Try not to worry too much, Erna. Heini will find help. He always does."

Heini is concerned whether today is the right time to ask his mother to help Brana. He sits quietly for a while. But his mother knows him too well.

"Is there something else you wanted to tell us, son?" She manages to smile again.

"Have you heard about poor Mrs Rosenbaum, Mother?"

"I have. One of my friends told me. Isn't it absolutely disgraceful?"

"It is, dangerous for us too. That's why we have to find somewhere to hide Brana, Mother."

He tells them how Horst suggested to send Brana to the fake-funeral of an imaginary sister in Dortmund to fool the neighbours and then hide her somewhere.

"Remember that old room of mine in the attic, Mother? Well, not really a room, is it? Still, it might be a safe hiding place for Brana. Nobody would ever look there, I hope. What do you think?"

"Nobody knows she is Jewish, Heini. I never told anyone. People think she is Polish, don't they? Is it really necessary?"

"Better safe than sorry. Things are escalating. Look at our poor Erna. Who would ever have thought..."

"If you are sure. You sort things out, but be careful!"

Heini is well aware of the danger he is putting his mother and sister in and the rest of the family. He has to make more than sure all of them are safe. He is also banking on Horst, his Nazi brother-in-law, to help somehow. It was his idea to hide Brana after all.

"Don't tell your friends, you two! You can't trust anyone any more."

During the next week Heini secures the space in the attic for Brana. It is only a very small place. He was happy there as a boy.

His bed is still up there, also a small wardrobe, a tiny table and a chair, all hidden by a wooden wall behind long washing lines. He used to love the clean smell of the washing drying there. There is no door. You have to know how to move that wall to get in. And if they all bring old sheets and other bits and pieces for the washing lines it should make the hideout even safer.

Of course, it will be very hard for Brana to be cooped-up there. And for how long? Nobody knows. She has always loved the outdoors. But Erna is bound to help her and the family can still come to see her, pretending that they are visiting Elizabeth and Erna.

Grandma Elizabeth   **Erna**   **Grandma Brana**

12

It is November 1st. All Saints Day. The words and Irmi are always deeply sad on this day. But they force themselves to be cheerful because Wonderful is coming and Irmi wants to tell him about the unique *Allerheiligen Kirmes,* All Saints Fair in Susato, which starts during the first week in November. It is the largest, most impressive Town-Centre-Fun-Fair in all of Europe.

She is sending the words away, tells them to hide until later when it is getting dark and Wonderful has left.

"Sadness has to wait, but I promise I'll call you later."

She can see his small boat from the window. His father is no longer sick. Wonderful has decided to bring her provisions from now on, especially during the cold months. His father is getting too old.

Irmi likes Wonderful. Lately he stays for a while, especially when she tells him about happy times in Susato. And there he is, struggling with lots of bags. A log-fire makes the room cosy and warm. Just right for him to thaw out. She opens the door. An icy wind stops her from smiling.

"Quick, quick, you must be frozen!" He is wet through.

"Just leave the bags there. I'll sort them later. Let me have your wet clothes. They should dry in no time by the fire."

He still hasn't said a word, looks exhausted, cold.

"Sit there in my favourite armchair by the fire. I'll make us some herb tea."

"Thanks."

His smile is false. Holding his hands close to the fire, thinking he should refuse to come. Why does she have to live here alone, even in winter. What if she was sick? Nobody to look after her. Madness!

"Here you are, my Wonderful. This should do the trick."

Placing the tea-tray on the rug she sits close to him on a small stool. "No wonder they have this fantastic, yearly town-centre fair in Susato in November. It is a miserable month."

"What's so good about that fair? I'm not all that keen on that sort of thing."

"Well, it has a long tradition, reaching as far back as 1417, maybe even further. St. Petri, the oldest church in town, was consecrated on All Saints Day, a good enough reason to celebrate for a whole week."

"You are joking, a whole week?"

"A pleasant change for the poor of that time but also for many local traders. Even traders from Holland, Scandinavia and the Baltic States came to enjoy it all, story-tellers, puppeteers, tightrope-walkers, carousels and lots more. Which would you have liked?"

"Not sure."

"My favourite was always the *Hall of Mirrors*. Do you know it?" She is looking at him. Is he interested at all? His beautiful, thick red hair is starting to gleam again. She needs to touch it.

"Let's see whether your hair is drying. You should wear a woolly hat, you know."

She strokes his hair and laughs. He seems to like it.

"Then there is that Horse-Market on a Thursday during that same week, selling horses, sheep, poultry etc. Mind you, it has changed a lot since, hardly any horses or livestock now. Do you like horses?"

"Not particularly."

"Horse-Market Day has always been a day for people to get roaring drunk with the help of *Bullen Auge,* Bull's Eye, a very special drink."

He is dozing off. She gets a blanket.

"Sleep, go on, sleep! It'll do you good. I'll tell you about the Bull's Eye later. It is a concoction invented during a meeting of the *Hellweg Dairy,* would you believe. Wish I had some to give to you now. Sweet dreams!"

He has been asleep for an hour. She put a soft cushion under his head stroking his hair again, softly, very softly not to wake him.

Am I getting too fond of this red-head? she is thinking, frightened. *Why shouldn't I? It is not going to change anything.*

"I was dreaming of your Bull's Eye."

He stretches his legs, takes his shoes off.

"Fibber! Do you want to hear more then?"

"Why not? Might as well get drunk simply by listening to your tale."

"Well, it is like this. During their meeting they ran out of *Schnapps,* only one bottle of *Mocha Liqueur* left. So they added a dash of double cream to every glass of *Mocha* and started to enjoy this new drink. Too much, of course!"

"The mixture doesn't sound very appetising."

"Maybe not, but after a while they all thought that a bull's eye in their glass was twinkling at them. So, that was the birth of the Susato *Bullen Auge,* which is even today the traditional, most important drink of the All Saints Fair."

"Why don't you pack a bag and go back to that fair in your hometown? Don't you ever get homesick? I'll take you across."

"No, no, all that has been dealt with long ago. But thanks just the same."

It is dark now and has stopped raining, the wind still howling though. Wonderful is getting ready to leave, disappointed really. He simply does not understand this woman.

After he has left she calls the words to help her cope with her emotions.

"Wonderful thinks I should visit the fair in Susato. What do you think?"

"It's up to you. Did he want to come with you?"

"I was worried about that at first, but then he didn't seem all that interested anyway. But I did enjoy remembering it all with him just the same."

13

The words have been waiting patiently. As always they want to help Irmi but are not looking forward to sharing her November sadness.

It is dark now. Irmi places burning candles all around her wild garden. There is frost on the ground but the wind has stopped howling. She tells the words to come closer.

"You know, *All Saints Day is* the day when Catholics in Susato go to the cemetery to light special candles on the graves of their loved ones."

Irmi does not believe in religion any more but growing up in a place with a *glorious* past where people are still trying to prove that *King Attala* came to Susato with his second wife *Kriemhild,* all based on the *Thidreksaga,* the Nordic version of the Germanic *Nibelungen Saga,* has instilled in her a love for old traditions and customs.

And a glorious past it was. Or was it? Here are the historical *facts.*

Susato with its own legal system was the very first town to have one which defined jurisdiction for a permanent market (now on Tuesday, Thursday and Saturday morning) and guaranteed the municipal peace, both internally and externally. The first law was written on a cow-hide. It still exists today. By 1270 the law had expanded to 130 articles. One was especially important for the growth of the town.

Anyone living in the vicinity of Susato must pay a town tax, together with 49 villages which are part of the district.

"Impressive, isn't it?" She is testing the words.

"Yes, but what about all those wars?" a group of cynics wants to know.

"Of course, of course, clever clogs! Let's look at what the history books say."

Defeat and devastation for Susato during the *Thirty Years War (1618-1648)* and after the *Seven Years War (1756-1763)* between Prussia and France when 50,000 Prussians clashed with 110,000 French soldiers before the gates of Susato. This proved too much for the already impoverished and destroyed town, losing more than half of its population. And yet, Susato always found ways to survive, to rebuild and start afresh.

"You know, it is said, often with much pride, that it is the sheer doggedness of the Westphalian character which helped to overcome adversity."

There is one victory Susato celebrates with pride and laughter, even today, the *Fehde 1444.*

The Susato citizens declared a feud with the archbishop of Cologne, their ruler at that time, to free themselves from his power and tax demands in order to decide their own destiny.

The archbishop's battle plan was that his 15,000 attacking mercenaries should weaken the defence of the Susato citizens behind their strong, protective town walls and fortified battle towers. No food supplies should enter through the then ten town-gates, aiming to starve the citizens into surrender.

But that plan did not succeed. Instead the archbishop's troops ended up starving while they were bombarded with boiling oil and refuse. Also, their ladders were too short for the high ramparts.

"Enough of your history lesson, my friends, but one story about this battle is told with a smile about the Mayor's wife who showed her bare, buxom bottom over the wall to let the enemy know that it would take a long time to starve them out."

"Is that true?"

"Does it really matter? Unfortunately after their victory things went downhill because Susato was now allied with the *Duchy of Kleve-Mark* and drawn into a war of succession. In *1616* the town was conquered for the first time in its history."

The words interrupt suddenly.

"Aren't you forgetting the Second World War?"

Irmi wishes she could. She battled to come to terms with it all her life. The facts in Susato are: 1,300 dead, 1,438 houses destroyed and most churches severely damaged.

Irmi is a child during that time. Later on as a young adult she wants answers but the subject is taboo, even in schools. Nobody talks. Most people are touchy about the Hitler Years, especially about the murder of the Jews. They still are, even today. Why? Many unanswered reasons, shame, guilt, anger, even a sense of betrayal.

"Leave it alone, Irmi!" is her family's attitude.

Osthofentor

For Irmi Susato's proud and glorious past ends with finding out about one particular incident, the night of the 9-10 of November when the Jewish School and Synagogue in *Osthofenstrasse* are burned to the ground by Nazis. Today, only a small plaque fastened to the house next door reminds the citizens of that night.

Here stood the Synagogue and School of the Jewish Community destroyed by the Nazis on Nov 9th 1938

How ironic, that the *Osthofentor,* the only still existing town-gate, a museum now, with an exhibition of 25,000 cross-bolts, is only a minute's walk away from where the Synagogue and School once stood. In the past those gates protected their citizens. That night they betrayed them forever.

Irmi has put a warm coat on, hat and gloves. She takes an old storm lamp and candles and asks the words to come with her.

"We have to bring some pebbles from the beach!"

Under a tired Judas tree, abandoned, almost flush with the ground at the mercy of wind and rain, two graves. Two mysteries, pilgrims perhaps returning from the *Holy Land,* struck down by *Black Death.* The stone carvings are unusual, one a lattice pattern under a figure with crossed arms, the other, a rope running the length of the coffin stone. Here, history stalks. The air shivers, only the cry of a curlew, bleak. The wind now keener watches dead, frosty leaves flapping along the ground until a secret fragrance brings fragile calm to a lonely night. These two graves haunt Irmi's imagination. She pretends that she is in Susato at the graves where Grandma Brana and Farmer Moller lie together. She places the pebbles on the graves and lights the candles.

Adieu you two, forever a part of me
Now, apart for ever and ever
Visit my heart
Remain close
Now, and for ever and ever

The words are quiet now. Irmi sits on a stone under the tree with its own scars of love. The candles are flickering. The words come close and stroke her heart, humming...

As for man the days are like grass

With the flowers of the field they flourish

The wind passes over their graves, taking them away

And the place shall know them no more

But let their names be blessed for ever and all eternity

The sun shall no more go down, neither shall the moon withdraw itself

For there will be everlasting light

14

Both Sarah and Toba work for Farmer Moller now. Toba doesn't really like working on a farm. She absolutely hates the pigs.

"Filthy things. How can anyone like them?"

But she doesn't mind the chickens and the colourful cockerel makes her laugh. Sarah helps her as always. Farmer Moller doesn't ask questions about Brana anymore, missing her, yes, but realizing that there is something secret he shouldn't know. He is a good man who continues to be kind to the sisters. They still live in the small house in *Stiftstrasse* and visit their mother often. There is concern about Brana now because she has lost a lot of weight in her hide-out. As always she does not complain, filling her time with knitting socks and baby clothes for Yetta and Heini's baby which is due any day now.

Erna looks after her really well, even keeping her company when it is safe to do so, in spite of her own heartache. There is one day of real panic in Grandma Elizabeth's house.

Bang, bang, bang! Someone is breaking the front door down. Two uniforms march into the living room shouting:

"Where is she? We have to take her away."

Elizabeth thinks they have found out about Brana. She calls her daughter who has just run up to the attic to hide Brana behind the wall. Coming down she is roared at:

"Are you Erna Lange?"

"I am."

"We've come to take you away."

"Take me away, why?"

"You did not reply to our letter to make an appointment with our doctors."

"I was sick."

"Liar, get your coat!"

Elizabeth is in shock. "What will you do to my daughter?"

"Never you mind. We should be taking you as well, you old, useless cripple. You are the living proof of everything Hitler is trying to put right now."

Erna is frightened for herself and her mother but also relieved that they haven't come for Brana.

"Don't you worry Mother. I am only seeing the doctors. I'll be back soon."

One of the neighbours sees that Erna is taken away. She is one of Hitler's converts and needs to find out why.

"It's nothing Mrs Becker. Thanks for asking. Erna has only been taken to the hospital. Some infectious thing or other, I believe. You better go home, not to catch anything."

That was quick thinking. It worked. This dangerous neighbour never called again.

Erna was sterilized, never to have children of her own. She never heard from her fiancé Franz again. Heini had been unable to help her after all. What kind of humiliating questions must poor Erna have had to endure? She refuses to talk about it. Perhaps she confides in Brana as they are both victims of the Hitler madness.

They separated her in more than just a gynaecological sense when even Ruth, her unhappy relative, thought:

"It might have been for the best, you know. They are oversexed these ... you know ... people. She has been seen in the fields with different men. The shame of it for the family."

Mind you, why be surprised? There are many who still have these or similar views today. Only their reasons are different from those of Hitler. Or are they? You know what, they say that money is the root of all evil, possibly, but even worse is ignorance.

The baby arrived on a Sunday. Children born on a Sunday are special, so they say. But it isn't a boy. It is Irmi. Yetta does not touch or look at the tiny girl with jet-black hair. Why? Because she wanted to please Heini who is replacing her first love, the adored father she lost as a young girl. She so wanted to give him *his boy,* not a girl. It was a difficult birth, leaving her quite weak. A good enough excuse to give the baby to Sarah. The always helpful sister asked Farmer Moller could she bring the little bundle with her for a while. It wouldn't be in the way of her work she promised.

So, little Irmi ends up in Sarah's and Toba's care, nearly for good. Yetta makes one illness-excuse after another not to have Irmi with her. Heini visits his daughter as much as he can. He knows she is in good hands. He loves her, plays with her, unaware of Yetta's real reasons.

"Thanks Sarah and you Toba for helping out. Yetta is not well at all. Wish I could do more but they have put me in charge of the ammunitions factory now."

"Irmi is fine, Heini. Just look at her. We love having her here."

"You know, they took me away for three days, trying to intimidate me, even threatening me because I refused to join the Nazi Party."

"Heini, be careful! As you know, people disappear all the time."

"I know. Yetta was out of her mind. She thought I would never come back either like dear Mrs Rosenbaum."

"Poor Yetta. Tell her to come and see us as soon as she is feeling better. She'll be surprised how much Irmi has grown."

"They need me, you see, now that Hitler has marched into Poland. Ironic, isn't it, but much better than poor Horst, the soldier, who will be forced to kill very soon. And yet, am I not killing just the same, providing the ammunition? Wars, again and again. Why?"

Farmer Moller comes in with a bottle of home-brew. "Not bad this year, Heini. Take it with you."

In spite of the war starting in Poland Yetta is determined to give Heini *his boy*. She is pregnant again not long after Irmi's birth.

Horst is on his way to the war, deeply troubled to leave Ruth and Clara, also because Ruth is now pregnant with his child.

"You know, how happy I am about the baby. Thank you, my love. Don't worry about a thing. I'll be back. Nothing is going to happen to me, not now. My child needs a father."

Ruth's feelings towards him have not changed. She pretends to care because she is frightened. Wartime on her own with two young children.

"Of course, you'll be back. Soon, I hope. We'll look after each other, my sisters and I. Also, Mother seems reasonably safe where she is. Don't forget to write. I will too."

Clara is crying.

"I don't want you to go, Papa. It is too far away."

He picks her up, strokes her hair. "You look after Mama for me. You are my big girl now."

" I will Papa, I will."

There is already one war casualty. Farmer Moller's nephew Otto, not fatal thankfully. He is on his way to his uncle to recover on his farm.

"Girls, sort out the big room for him, the one with the grandfather clock. He always liked it. He should be here by tomorrow. You'll like him. I always have."

Otto arrives early. He is a handsome young man, tall, perhaps a little too pale and tired-looking in his uniform. He is limping. Sarah is the first to greet him, takes his army rucksack.

"Come in, and sit here in your uncle's favourite armchair. Coffee is on its way. Do you like plum tart?"

"You bet."

The door opens, Toba with a large tray and his uncle with a broad smile.

"So glad you are here, boy. Let's sit at the table and have something to eat. Tell us all about it. Are you in pain?"

"Not too bad, uncle. Thanks for having me. Where did you find these beautiful girls?"

They laugh.

"They'll spoil you. You'll soon be yourself again, climbing up that old plum tree as you used to do as a boy."

"Very soon, I hope."

He smiles at the sisters. For Sarah it is love at first sight. She blushes, dares not look at him. And Toba? She likes him too.

15

It is December 6th. *Saint Nikolaus Day.* The words are refusing to play. They want Irmi to talk to Wonderful instead. It is about time she made more of an effort because he is starting to like her. Also, they want a day flying free without Irmi and her sad and furious tales.

It is a frosty day, the fire in the living room blazing. Irmi has baked her aunt Sarah's special cake. Yes, it is true, she depends too much on the words for company, thinking:

Why not talk to him and get to know my Wonderful better? I know so little about him.

And there he comes, wearing a new, red, woolly hat. It makes her laugh. She runs towards him to help with the bags, still laughing.

"What's so funny?"

"You look wonderful, Mr Wonderful. That hat is completely you."

"Thought you might like it. Wait till you see the one I brought for you."

They dump the bags in the middle of the room. Wonderful heads straight for the fire-place, rubbing his hands.

"You need gloves now. Red ones to match your hat."

They laugh again. He pulls her hat out of his coat pocket. It is the same as his. She puts it on, smiling.

"Thank you, my Wonderful. I will not take it off for at least a week."

He has taken his coat off, not his hat. There they are, the hat-twins, happy.

"My new house rule from now on will be: if you want a cup of coffee and a piece of cake, you have to wear a red hat. Okay?"

Wonderful has pulled the old, comfy armchair close to the fire. He told his dad that he might be home later than usual, hoping that Irmi would let him stay a while.

"What is that lovely smell, like cinnamon?"

"I baked a cake for this special day."

"What special day?"

"It's *Saint Nikolaus Day*. Don't you know?"

"No, so what?"

"Didn't he come to your house when you were a boy?"

"No, who and why?"

"Well, I'll tell you what happened in our house on the 6th of December every year. But first, let's relax, have some coffee."

And there they sit, warm and smiling at each other, Irmi next to him on the mat. This is what she tells him:

"On December 6th during the war my father asked two of his work-mates from the ammunition factory to come to our house dressed as *Saint Nikolaus* and *Knecht Ruprecht*. My brothers and I were waiting for that knock at the door. My youngest brother Fritzchen was terrified, hiding under the table, only lifting the table-cloth now and then, shouting real loud: *Who wants those stale biscuits and candis-sugar anyway? Not me.*

"He was a lively boy, always in trouble. You would have liked him. When we were all dressed up in our Sunday best, ready to visit the relatives, he ended up in the middle of a puddle catching raindrops with his mouth wide open."

"A boy with a mind of his own. I like him already."

"Very much so. He always refused to blow up the frogs in our garden, with a straw, until they popped."

"Did you?"

"Don't look at me! Yes, I did. And another thing. Fritzchen always covered the canary's birdcage with a table-cloth as soon as

57

the sirens went off. Then he whispered to the bird: *Don't you worry now! The bombers cannot see you under there. But you mustn't sing. Promise!* He hated *Kindergarten* because he had to wear the shoes of his older brother Klaus which were much too big for him. Wartime, you see. Mind you, he could sing, had a lovely, clear voice. There was this one song he loved:

On a tree a cuckoo sat

SIM SALA BIM SAM BASALA DUSALA DIM

On a tree a cuckoo...

It was the SIM SALA BIM he repeated over and over again with much joy.

"Go on, sing it for me!"

She does, embarrassed, taking his hand.

"Join me, come on! SIM SALA BIM..."

He does, laughing.

"We only ever sang the first verse because in the last verse the cuckoo is shot down by a hunter, dead. Fritzchen thought that was absolutely disgraceful."

"What a boy!"

Wonderful, acting out the fate of the hunter's cuckoo, is lying on the rug now, dead. Irmi joins him. But both are not quite sure, should they laugh? Wonderful breaks the awkward silence.

"Anything else to tell me?"

They go over to the table. Irmi brings her cake in.

"I'm slimming, thanks."

"You simply have to try this. I cannot eat it all myself."

They are smiling at each other again.

"Do you want me to tell you what happened next?"

"Of course."

"Well, there was that knock at the door. In came *Saint Nikolaus* with his long, white beard, much like a Father Xmas today, opening his big, red book where all our good and bad deeds were written down. We were praised for our good deeds and received biscuits and candis-sugar, the only so-called sweets for children during the war. Do you know who *Knecht Ruprecht is?*"

"No, not at all."

"That year he was a fearful, scruffy looking man who smelt of beer, carrying a large, dirty sack and waving a stick about. Any small child would have been frightened of him. He had come to punish us for our bad deeds or at least threatened to do so. Fritzchen was still hiding under the table when *Knecht Ruprecht* shouted real loud: *Come out from under there! You are the naughtiest boy in town. I will have to take you away in my big sack!*"

"Your poor brother! How cruel!"

"I know. He did come out, very, very slowly, tears streaming down his little, white face. But suddenly he stormed against his tormentor, pushed him over with such a force you would not have expected in such a small boy. The man stumbled. Fritzchen dashed to the door just at that moment when the sirens went off. My parents ran after him calling, calling: *Fritzchen, Fritzchen, wait for us!*"

"*Knecht Ruprecht* sneaked to the toilet. We could hear him being sick. The kind Father Xmas gave us a hug: *Fritz will be fine. We have to go to the shelter now. You two come with me!*"

"Go on, go on! What happened?"

Irmi is not sure whether to tell him. He looks at her, worried but needing to know.

"It's important that you tell me."

"That night our baby brother was found dead."

Irmi has taken her red hat off. Wonderful does the same.

"I am so glad your parents didn't bother with *Saint Nikolaus Day*. Perhaps some people hold on to certain traditional customs to give them a sense of security during times of upheaval. What do you think?"

He is sitting close to her, holding her hand.

"So sorry about that lovely brother of yours. You see, I was in America during the war. My mother's sister took me. I didn't know why at that time. Only that my mother was very sick and couldn't travel. Dad had to look after her but promised they would join us later."

"Did you like it in America?"

"I did, only I missed my parents. My aunt said that I would get a better education there, especially with the war starting in Germany."

"So, you don't have brothers or sisters?"

"No, just me."

Suddenly, he starts to cry. Irmi goes to him, holding him real close, kissing his hair.

"What is it, my Wonderful?"

A long silence.

"My Mum died too."

Irmi could have kicked herself for mentioning her brother. Too late! All they can do now is cry together.

16

The war is escalating and so is the bombing in Susato. The main target is an important railway junction for army and food supplies on the way to Berlin.

Completely in the wrong place, not far from that station is a very large shelter. Ruth and her girls, yes, she has two now, Clara and Baby-Mona, run to it day and night, often together with Toba and Irmi as they all live near by.

Listening to the sound of the bombers overhead there is worried talk about the very thick hot water pipes which run along the walls and ceilings of the building. What if a bomb hits even just part of it? These pipes are bound to burst and...

"We would not have a dog's chance!" one woman screams, holding her baby high up to show it to the other women.

"All right, all right, we know. Calm down! Look, what you have done."

All the children have started to cry. How hard it must have been for women with small children to cope on their own, their husbands away. Ruth hasn't heard from Horst for over three months.

Sarah stays with Otto and Farmer Moller in their large farmhouse cellar. They are worried that Otto might have his leg amputated. Sarah loves him with all her heart. Toba knows that he prefers her but is careful not to encourage him. She wants Sarah to be happy, the sister who always thinks of others first. Otto will need a good and patient nurse, and she knows that she could not be that person.

Grandma Elizabeth, Erna and Brana hide under the stairs when the sirens go off. It is cramped but they have put old bedclothes down and huddle together. There isn't a shelter nearby.

Anyway, Elizabeth cannot walk very far and Brana has to remain hidden. Erna does her best to make it as comfortable as she can for the two old ladies.

Since the tragic death of Fritzchen on *Saint Nikolaus Day,* Klaus is even more precious to Yetta now. She has forgotten her daughter Irmi altogether, or so it seems. Irmi is still looked after by Sarah and Toba, partly on the farm and partly in the small house in *Stiftstrasse.* As things tend to happen, on this particular day Irmi has come to see her mother and brother Klaus. The boy is happy to see her, someone to play with. But jealousy stops Irmi from being kind to her brother. She torments him until he starts to cry. Her mother is furious, slaps her across the face. She forces herself not to cry, laughs instead.

"Get your things! You are going back to Sarah and Toba!"

"It is getting dark, Mama."

"Never you mind, get ready! You know your way back. Get moving!"

Just at that moment the sirens go off. The house has a large cellar. People from the neighbourhood use it as their shelter.

"Quickly, quickly, into the cellar!"

Neighbours are already rushing in with young children, babies in prams and heavy bags, terrified. Yetta and her children have secured a place under a strong steel girder which is holding up part of the ceiling. Irmi has brought her candis-sugar.

"Don't let the other children see it. There isn't enough to go round."

The women start to talk nervously. As always they have brought their ever-ready flasks of hot drinks hoping, some praying, that this air-raid will be over soon and they can go home, that is, if their houses are still there.

One old man sits huddled in a corner. It could be that he was a soldier in the First World War. He is shaking.

"Don't you worry now, Mr Braun! It will soon be over again."

One woman hands him some coffee, *Muckefuck* of course. You can only get real coffee on the Black Market. Only now, people have few things left to trade in.

And then it happens.

Crash, bang, crash, the cellar is shaking. They can hear the sound of the bombers loud and clear. Someone screams: *Volltreffer! A* direct hit.

More screaming is coming from heads sticking out of a pile of rubble. Where the bomb has hit is a deep hole surrounded by mounds of bricks. Prams have been flung high up, stopped by partly remaining ceiling areas. Some of the children have disappeared altogether. Where are they? Only Yetta, Irmi and the boy are able to move about a little, saved by that strong girder. They are trying to remove some of the bricks to get at least the heads next to them freed. Difficult! It is much too dark and a heavy dust cloud makes breathing nearly impossible. Irmi puts her candis-sugar in one head's mouth. She probably saved that person's life.

The screaming of the babies high up in their prams is now unbearable.

"Please help them first! They are choking. The dust is suffocating them."

Too late. The screaming has stopped.

The old man is still alive, crawling to the only very narrow window-opening. The glass has shattered but iron bars make it impossible to get out. He is trying to scrape the bars loose with his fingers which are bleeding and he has a deep head wound.

"Come on, children, you have to shout real loud! Someone might hear us."

"Thank you, Mr Braun."

Yetta is hopeful.

"Everyone stay calm! I can hear movement outside."

The children suck their candis-sugar and keep on shouting until there is a voice from outside.

"We'll have you out very soon."

They are rescued, dug out, brick by brick. Sadly, not all of them. Yetta, Irmi, the boy Klaus and the old man Mr Braun are safe. When they are at last back out in the open, houses are burning all around. The sky is red and there is that now well known disaster smell.

Yetta begs the rescue-team, crying:

"Can I have a look whether there is anything left of our flat?"

"No, my dear, it's all gone. Sorry."

Suddenly, she spots her two *Paradekissen,* those very special, fashionable feather cushions for the bed she embroidered together with her sisters as part of her trousseau. She rushes over, climbs onto a heap of bricks to get them. How did they survive all this?

"Be careful! The house is still collapsing and burning. We have to go now. We will tell Heini that you are all safe so far."

They put the old man and other survivors on stretchers and take them all to some makeshift shelter. It must have been a strange sight when they arrive there, Yetta holding on to her large feather cushions.

The next morning, very early, Heini arrives to pick up his family with *a Bollerwagen,* a wooden cart with 4 wheels and a long handle to pull it along. They put the *Paradekissen* in and put the children on top.

"Where are we going?" Yetta wants to know.

"To one of the villages. Don't know which one yet. Not far, though."

"How far?"

"Ten kilometres, perhaps."

"You are joking, Heini. On foot?"

"Come on, start pulling!"

Heini smiles at the children. They like sitting high up on the cushions as their parents pull them through Susato in ruins. At every corner more and more people join the trek. In the end there must have been hundreds with carts, bikes and prams, all heading for the safer countryside, dragging along their few possessions.

Their destination is an old school house in a small village. Army bunk-beds have been put up in the school hall. People are pushing to get in first. It is all excitement for Irmi and her brother. They soon sit in a top bunk, playing. Yetta is exhausted, nearly falling asleep.

"I have to leave you now. Must find out what has happened to the rest of the family during this last air-raid. And they expect me back at the *FLAK*, the town's anti-aircraft defence. Back soon, I hope."

He kisses them.

"Bye, Papa. We like it here. Are we on holiday?"

"Of course, you are. Be good for Mama. You can have a look at the cows and lambs tomorrow."

The farmers of the area allow the refugees to dig out potatoes and vegetables from their fields and then there are the fruit trees, a source of pleasure, food and a playground for the children.

The accommodation is cramped with only one wood-fuelled *Kanonenofen,* a small, round all-black stove for all of them to cook on. The women often fight for their turn. There is water from the well. No soap, though.

Every now and then a farmer brings milk for the children. But not all farmers are so generous. There is one incident Yetta never forgot. She went to a farm nearby with her children to ask for some milk. As they walked towards the farmhouse they could smell baking.

"Children, how lucky! We will have a treat today. Can you smell it, waffles, your favourites?"

No way! The farmer chases them away, calling them dirty, no good beggars. Yetta promised herself to pay him back one day, shouting:

"I hope a bomb drops on your farm tonight!"

However, the farmer was right somehow. Their clothes are dirty, full of lice and the children's hair is infested too.

There is something else Yetta is particularly concerned about. Her children are far too young to witness so much sexual activity going on all around. The farm-hands are having a ball. They know what some women will do for just a few eggs. The children ask her questions she does not want to answer.

"Mama, the man in the bed over there is hurting the woman again. He is lying on top of her, squashing her until she makes funny noises. Is he trying to kill her?"

Yetta is waiting for Heini. Will he be able to come soon? She knows he is needed to be with the *FLAK*. There is always that next air-raid. But they simply have to get away from here. She is considering walking back with the children now, in spite of the danger.

17

Irmi has not seen Wonderful since his last red-hat-visit. His father brings her weekly provisions again, making excuses for him. She is surprised but also disappointed that she misses him, thinking:

Maybe it is better that he does not want to come anymore. I would only have to hurt him in the end, anyway. Solitude and the words, that's me. No room for anyone else.

She is preparing for her first Christmas here, alone. Did she have plans before to invite Wonderful to remember the good times during the festive season in Susato with him? The words are annoyed with her, tormenting her, offering sarcasm:

Snowdrops whitemail to the fold young customers and old.
Only to be sold bald hope and drink,
and greed-wrapped all in pink
peace on the brink.
Also, battery-timed joys from electronic toys.
Perfumed love and tinselled wonder,
all to make the soul grow fonder
of glitzy things
flown in on advertising wings
piloted by three well-known kings
Merry...

Yes, she agrees with all that. And yet, what she really wants are the bells of St. Petri to call her. Luckily they do, louder and louder.

It is Christmas Eve in Susato on a dark and icy night. Under the tower of the *Auld Kirk* more and more people are gathering. Woolly hats, scarves and heavy winter boots are moving closer together. Was it always this bitterly cold? All are looking up. When will it start? There, the first flickers of lantern lights from the church tower. So, they are up there. Should not be long now. Nobody speaks. Even the children are quiet. Snow is falling softly. At last, a sound of trumpets vibrates shakily into the night, sometimes loud and sometimes faint as the choir walks round and round the tower, singing:

Gloria in excelsis Deo

Many join in. Young and old voices celebrate this traditional Christmas Eve in Susato.

The children are the first to break the spell. Snowballs landing on friend and foe are much more important now. People have started to talk to each other. Many are looking forward to welcoming relatives and friends to their post-war festivities, to enjoy glorious food and drink and happy children with their new toys.

Just for a moment Irmi wonders how Wonderful used to spend his Christmas Eves, then forces herself not to think of him. Does it matter now? Solitude suits her. Nothing and nobody is going to spoil it. How can anyone understand, anyway. Nobody ever did.

Irmi has been baking Christmas biscuits. An old tradition in her family. As a child she always helped Sarah and Toba together with her cousins Clara and Baby-Mona. Only the war sirens spoiled their fun sometimes.

She has just put the Christmas biscuits on a large plate to cool when the door opens. It is Wonderful's father.

"Sorry, Miss, I am a little early this week. The shop is closing for the festive season. Thought I should bring at least two weeks supply. We are going away, you see, my son and I, visiting relatives."

"Thank you so much. Hope you have a lovely time. Would you like some of my Christmas biscuits? I'll put them in this box for you."

"That is very kind. We will certainly enjoy them."

"How is your son?"

What made her ask? She hates herself.

The father is embarrassed. Does not know what to say. Then suddenly, he changes his mind and it all comes bursting out.

"I so hoped you two would get on. My son is a loner, you see. I worry about him, no real friends, just his boat. He loves that boat. And I worry about you too. Here all alone, what if you got sick? But you must have good reasons to live as you do. Sorry!"

Now Irmi does not know what to say. She likes the man. He has a sad, rather worn but kind face and is much too thin.

"Don't you worry! I am fine. If you are not in a hurry, have a coffee with me. Sit over there by the fire! I love my fire, even during the summer months. Your son has stacked enough wood for me to keep it going for ever."

He smiles.

"I nearly forgot. My son asked me to give you this, to open on Christmas Eve. Not before, though."

It is a small parcel and a letter. Irmi is confused and guilty that she has not thought of a present for him. The father does not stay very long. It is just small talk between them now. Neither wants to intrude on the other's privacy by asking further questions. They simply wish each other a happy festive time and a healthy New Year.

After the father has left Irmi is dying to open Wonderful's present, especially the letter, but she forces herself not to.

I'll make a special day for me and the words by candle-light, eating my biscuits and listening to Christmas carols on the radio. I can wait. I will wait.

When it is Christmas Eve Irmi is excited like a child, opening Wonderful's present. Her first reaction is complete silence. Then, nervous laughter fills the room. She is stroking a pair of red, woolly gloves, just right to match her red hat.

"How wonderful, my Wonderful!"

But why is she so happy? Does it matter? She fetches the hat and puts the gloves on. There she sits, next to the radio as *Stille Nacht* creeps into her heart. Then comes the scary part, opening his letter.

My dear Fury,

So sorry I have not been to see you. You deserve an explanation. Our friendship is precious to me. However. I realised something important is missing. We never talk about ourselves, not really, although *we* started to at our last time together. It was painful but real, as it should be between friends or lovers.

There is so much you don't know about me. I need time to find out whether you are the person I can trust fully before I open up further. Maybe it is the same for you.

I am going to America for a while. Back in May. We'll see whether *we* are ready for more talks by then. I do hope so.

We are both outsiders, two difficult personalities with strong views on how things should be. Not an easy start for a good relationship. And most importantly, what sort of relationship do we both want? Nothing is clear yet, is it?

So, until then, take good care of yourself! Enjoy the spring! Hopefully, I'll miss you. That would clear the fog a little.

Wishing you a magical New Year

Your Wonderful

Irmi is confused.

I have to go for a walk. Maybe the cold air... Well, let's see.

She puts on her warmest coat and boots. Should she wear that red hat and the new gloves? She does. Why not?

Outside everywhere is white, the sky still, hiding the winter sun in a dazzling, brilliant haze. The trees are still frosted. The grass and the weeds in her garden are flattened by the sudden fall of snow, covering sand, gravel and stones near their beach. She needs to go there to be near him, listening to the waves as they did so many times together. Their rhythm should calm her mind; for now, that is.

18

After leaving Yetta and the children in the village Heini hurries to check on Ruth's house first. It is a complete ruin. Where are they? Maybe with Sarah and Toba in the small house in *Stiftstrasse.* He cannot get there quickly enough. Are they safe? He does know they always go to the shelter near the station, day or night, but you never know. How safe is that shelter?

As he comes around the corner, relief. At least that house is still standing. Ruth opens the door. The two little girls come running down the stairs.

"Uncle Heini, uncle Heini, our beds are all wringing wet. It rains through our ceiling."

"Wait a minute, girls! Let uncle Heini come in first."

"How bad is it, Ruth?"

"Very, very bad, it is draughty, wet and cold. All the windows are out, but at least we have somewhere to stay. For the moment that is."

"Where are the others?"

"Sarah and Toba are staying with Farmer Moller all the time now. He has been really good to all of us. But what about you? How are Yetta and the kids? I thought the world was coming to an end during the last air-raid."

Heini tells her what happened. Ruth is crying.

"They could have been killed, all of them. Heini, what have we ever done to deserve all this? We were in the shelter, thank God, but coming back to our bombed home, everything gone ... Well what can I say?"

She cannot stop crying. The girls hug her. Wipe her tears with a tea-towel.

"Mama, Mama, don't cry! It has stopped raining. We'll be very, very good going to bed tonight or to the shelter."

"Heini, did you lose everything too?"

"Not everything. Yetta rescued her two *Paradekissen.*"

They laugh in spite of everything. The girls join in, jumping up and down, laughing louder and louder. Does it matter that they do not really know why? It seems that very young children take even the hardest times in their stride. When they were asked many years after the war "How frightened were you during the bombing?" they said "It was more exciting than anything. But it must have been more than a nightmare for the adults. Terrifying. We know that now."

"Ruth, I have to go now to see Farmer Moller. I cannot leave Yetta and the children in that jam-packed school-house much longer. Do you remember that outhouse in the farmyard? Maybe...?"

"That is an idea. I wish you luck. He is a good man. If he can, he will help you. Heartbroken about his nephew. They did have to amputate the leg after all. Otto is back on the farm now. The hospital has been hit too. Sarah is looking after him day and night trying to get the fever down."

"Bye, girls. See you again very soon. I'll bring Irmi and the boy. Don't forget to look after Mama."

"We will, uncle Heini, but we want Papa to come home. Mama said that he must be well on his way by now."

Farmer Moller has two Polish *Strafarbeiter,* prisoners of war, to help him on the farm. A bomb hit part of the outhouse only yesterday where the two men used to sleep. Luckily, everybody was in the farmhouse cellar when it happened. At least, that house has been spared so far. Now the men are fixing the roof. As Heini enters the farmyard he can see even more damage. Will it be possible for his family to stay there? How long will all the repairs take?

Farmer Moller is feeding the chickens when Heini arrives.

"Heini, I am over here. Thought you were shooting the bastards down with your defence aircraft spotters."

"No chance. We are running out of ammunition."

"When is this hell going to end, Heini?"

"Never, so Hitler says. He is still winning the war."

"Some fools in Susato believe that too. But never mind all that now. How is your family?"

"That is why I am here, Farmer Moller. I need your help."

Again he is telling what happened to their home in *Thomästrasse* and about the trek to the village. Farmer Moller is speechless.

"Come with me to the pig sty. Let us see what can be done to help. See Sarah and Toba later. I am so grateful that they are here, helping my nephew Otto."

"Ruth told me about him. I am so sorry."

"So am I. A young man's life ruined. For what, Heini, a mad man's ego-trip?"

They pass the outhouse. His heart sinks.

"Thought there might be some room in there for us until I find something else."

"There is, Heini. As you can see, the two Polish workers are fixing things at the moment. Only, they would have to stay with you, nowhere else to go either and I am responsible for them. They are good lads. Know all about farming. Never complain about their lot."

"Don't know how to thank you, Farmer Moller. Hope to make it up to you one day."

"Come on, let's go into the cellar and surprise the sisters! We are living there permanently now, all of us together. Mind you, the sisters have turned it into a warm home, war or no war. They are even decorating the cellar for Christmas. Women, eh! What would we do without them?"

Heini is close to crying. He misses Yetta and the children. Not long now and they will be sorting the outhouse out together, hoping that a bomb will not hit the same place twice. Tomorrow, tomorrow, he will pick them up tomorrow. Sod the FLAK! Let them wait.

"Toba, look Toba, who is here!"

"Heini, we have been so worried. Where are Yetta and the kids?"

"That is a long story but they are safe."

"Come and sit here and tell us all about it. Are you hungry?"

"Always. Nothing has changed there."

It does not take long before they serve a full meal, potatoes, *Sauerkraut* and meat, even a bottle of home brew.

"Is it still wartime, girls?"

The sisters smile.

"Not today, Heini. Enjoy it while it lasts!"

Then he tells them in detail what happened. When they hear that Farmer Moller has offered to help again, both go over and hug him. He likes it. Never had a wife. Looked after his sick, old mother instead for many years. Only Brana helped him.

"Heini, you can tell Yetta we are planning a wonderful family Christmas, all of us, here in the cellar. We can, can't we, Farmer Moller?"

"Of course, girls. Let us forget the bombs. Heini is going to shoot the beggars down anyway."

"How is Otto, Sarah?"

"Still very feverish, but we are getting there. He is asleep at the moment. I do not want to wake him. Speak to him when you come back with Yetta and the kids. Soon, I hope."

"Very soon, Sarah. Yetta will be so happy to see you all again, safe and sound."

"Have you been in touch with Elizabeth, Erna and Brana?"

"The house did not look too bad. They seem to be coping so far. Mind you, that was a few days ago."

Heini leaves. They cannot see that he is crying. What a family! And that farmer, what a man! Ten kilometres on foot, so what? He will soon be there. Half-way he sees three bedraggled people walking towards him. It can't be Yetta? It is. The kids have spotted him first.

"Papa, Papa, we are coming home."

"Heini, I could not stay there any longer. Just look at us, dirty, worn out and itchy, full of lice."

"No need to stay there any more, Yetta. We'll all be fine now."

Yetta is crying, aware and grateful that Heini is able to be there to look after them. Not like so many women on their own now. Hand in hand they walk on, not very fast, tired, but together, Irmi and her brother Klaus running ahead.

Yetta is overjoyed that her sisters are safe.

"That Farmer Moller is special. Even my father would have been impressed. We all knew his opinion about rich farmers generally, remember? Mind you, he would have been right about one farmer here. Wait until I tell you that story. And what about Brana, Erna and your mother?"

"As soon as I have taken you to the farm I am going to see them. They were safe a few days ago. Just had to come and fetch you first.

"Where are your *Paradekissen?* I told them, you know. Your sisters laughed and laughed and laughed."

Yetta stops and kisses him.

"The bugs invaded them. Good riddance!"

The sisters are shocked when they see the three of them. Off with their clothes, which are burned right away and a large iron bath-tub is put in front of the fire.

"Just look at the children's hair!"

Toba has an idea.

"We simply cut it all off, shave it even and tell them it is the latest fashion. Brana has already crocheted Christmas hats for them. They can wear those now."

In later years Irmi always remembered how her hair grew back very slowly, sticking through the tiny crochet-holes in the hat.

Yetta's hair is washed with vinegar. Vinegar, the magic lotion to cure all, especially the bug bites.

Before Heini leaves to see to the other relatives, Farmer Moller takes him to one side.

"They are all invited for Christmas, don't forget. I am looking forward to a jolly cellar family-do. Something unique, don't you think?"

The two men smile and shake hands. What else can they do? So, Farmer Moller did know about Brana. Heini is not surprised. He must have guessed all along. It is probably safe to bring her with them now. This war cannot last much longer. Or can it?

When Heini arrives at his mother's he finds the three fast asleep under the stairs. What a sight! They soon wake up when they hear his voice.

"Heini, Heini, where have you been?"

"Keeping the bombers away from your house. But never mind about that now. You are all invited to a family Christmas with a difference. You will have plenty to talk about. I'll pick you up Christmas morning. Till then, have a good snooze. Things can only get better."

Soon Heini and his family are trying to set up home in the outhouse. The Polish workers are a great help. They have moved spare beds from the farmhouse. Nobody lives there any more. It is all very basic, but home.

It is Christmas morning. Heini has borrowed an old army jeep to pick up his relatives.

"Back in an hour," he tells his comrades. "Can't see them bombing us today."

All three are waiting, dressed in their Sunday best, excited. They do not know where Heini is taking them. The shock as they make their way through a town in ruins. Nobody talks.

Arriving at the farm they see that all are safe, even happy. The sisters worked endlessly to make this the best Christmas ever. It is time for the special celebration meal.

"Come on children, let's all sit at the table!"

It is a long table with a pure white tablecloth. On it stands Brana's antique *Menorah,* a candelabra which simply appeared one day, many, many years ago.

"A present from a friend," was all Brana ever said. Today no longer her secret with a very special meaning. Sarah lights all the candles and smiles at her mother.

The Polish men make their way to the door but Farmer Moller stops them.

"No, no, there is enough food for all of us. Go and sit next to Brana! Have a chat in your own language!"

Brana is happy to talk to them. Questions, questions, questions. Where are they at home in Poland? Have they a wife, children? One man shows her a photo of his son and daughter. He looks so proud. The other man is very quiet, looks sad, close to tears. Both of them are surprised that Brana comes from their homeland. They have many questions too. But of course, Brana has still to be careful not to give too much away. Did they notice the *Menorah?*

It is a heart-warming Christmas. Otto is brought in. The children sit on his bed showing him their new, modest toys. He is telling them stories from when he was a boy here on the farm. But Heini's son wants to know about the war.

"Did you shoot people, uncle Otto?"

Sarah joins them. She looks so happy.

"No, no Klaus, they shot Otto because they had to. It is all so very wrong. War makes some people do horrible things."

The girls have been listening.

"Uncle Otto, do you think Papa might come today to surprise us?"

"Maybe, girls. You never know."

The Polish man with a son and daughter is wiping his eyes. Ruth is still waiting to hear from Horst. Is he still alive?

The meal is excellent. Farmer Moller has killed one of his pigs. The roast pork is a real treat together with winter vegetables from Sarah's cottage garden. And of course, homemade cakes in the afternoon.

The sisters are still teasing Yetta about her *Paradekissen*.

"Never mind, they can be replaced. But who could replace the unique you?"

Elizabeth and Erna are comfortable on the old sofa, not saying very much, just listening and smiling.

"Come on, let us sing, all of us!" Toba shouts.

"Without you, Toba."

They laugh, remembering how she always spoiled their singing on summer evenings in their family home in the *Stiftstrasse*.

"I have practised since then," she defends herself. As in the past, nothing is going to stop her.

0 TANNENBAUM, 0 TANNENBAUM, wie grün sind deine Blätter.

Oh CHRISTMAS TREE, Oh CHRISTMAS TREE, how green your leaves are

The children love it and dance with Farmer Moller. The boy is not joining in.

"I am not dancing. It's sissy."

The girls grab him and kiss him. He is furious, embarrassed, shouting: "Don't you ever do that again, you silly girls!"

Farmer Moller takes him to one side.

"Let's all have some of my apple-wine. I've hidden it. Come with me, Klaus! You have to carry it."

The Christmas day ends with a great surprise. Sarah and Otto are sitting on his bed, holding hands.

"You are all invited to our wedding as soon as this war madness is over."

Screams from the sisters. Congratulations all around. What a wonderful Christmas day it has been! No sirens to spoil their day either. Farmer Moller jokes:

"I wish someone would have me."

Somehow everyone noticed that he was looking at Brana, lovingly.

Happy Christmas   **Happy Chanukah**
And a peaceful New Year without war.

19

It has been a long, cold waiting time for Irmi. Even her word-companions are silent. Melancholy wishes the winter to retreat, allowing spring to creep in cautiously so that not even the snowdrops feel the cold. Dulled senses seek solace in shy, slanting sun rays and long shadows on coarse grass. Already light, rust and white petals stroke Irmi's tired, old oak tree to re-kindle pleasure in its new, bursting life. Warm, heavy love-drops rush down and drown dry, yearning wood. Fresh power flirts with winter's hurt of doomed, rotting roots. There is hope again in the tree's strong, greening arms.

Will the swelling seas entice elves, hidden away in her woodland for millions of years to rescue the mystery of love? Or will Irmi let it all drown again, pregnant with anger, confusion and disappointment at the first taste of pollution?

She is waiting for Wonderful's father to bring her groceries and perhaps news from his son in America. He is staying longer than usual lately. She spoils him with coffee and cakes. He enjoys her treats. They still don't talk an awful lot but smile at each other all the time, embarrassed perhaps. Irmi knows how much he misses his son. And what about her? Does she miss him too? She does but remains frightened and unsure what that could mean.

Let us be patient, my Wonderful! There is bound to be an honest answer for both of us when you are back here in May.

This is just one way to console herself when the waiting puts a strain on her jumbled thoughts.

There, his father is coming up the rugged path. He walks slowly, looks old and tired. The bags are much too heavy for him.

"Hello there. Let me help you." She hurries towards him.

"I am getting old, my dear, but never mind, my son is on his way home. He sent you a postcard. Here it is, New York. I am certain he will be glad to get back, away from the hectic life of the *Big Apple.*"

Both smile. Inside, he heads for the armchair, looks quite at home already. Irmi is happy about that.

"I brought you a present. Look!"

It is a beautiful painting.

"My island on canvas. How lovely!"

"Glad you like it. My grandfather, a famous painter who loved this island, painted it. He lived here all alone, like you, for many years. Bought this tiny, sacred place for a song and our family inherited it. However, we had to promise that only very special people should share it with us. His earnest wish was:

It is only for people who need to be on their own. People who embrace solitude.

"I never understood what he meant, not really. But I am certain, he would have approved of you being here."

"What a surprise! A person who knew about solitude."

"So far we have been able to honour his wish with one sad exception. During the Hitler Years the island was invaded by the military. Nothing was sacred at that time. Might is right! Always will be, I suppose."

Irmi does not comment. She is surprised how easily he is talking to her today. It must be Wonderful's homecoming. She is happy for him.

"Another thing I wanted to tell you. Our village is celebrating their annual *Schützenfest,* Rifle Club Festival. Were you ever part of it in your hometown?"

"Very much so, especially as a young girl after the war. We had lots of fun. My cousins and I learning to dance in a large Festival Tent with wet soil squelching through the wooden floor boards."

She coughs with laughter remembering those days.

"By evening we looked absolutely filthy. Wet muck all over our sandals, socks and special party clothes."

"It sounds hilariously filthy."

"Funny, it always rained, every year. We didn't care. Learned how to waltz ... one two three... one two three ... hiccupped, bloated with *Dunkelbier,* a malt children's beer with only a very small alcohol content."

"Thank you my dear, for sharing that happy time with me. I could see you doing the dirty waltz, honest, I could. Sorry, that I have to go home now. Get the house ready for him. He'll probably see you very soon with exciting tales from New York. Take care! Also thanks for all your tasty cakes. Did you notice how greedy I am? I ate them all."

Irmi walks with him to the boat, waves goodbye, thinking: *Yes, they were happy times those days with my cousins during the Rifle Club Festival. Wonder whether Wonderful can waltz. If he can't, I'll teach him.*

She is smiling. So, her Wonderful is coming home. To calm her emotions she puts the radio on. Music always helped. Unfortunately it is march music, not really what she wanted but is not surprised when it takes her straight back to the main Rifle Club Festival in her hometown.

There she is, enjoying that spectacular parade again as Rifle Club members march to loud and powerful music on their way to the Market Square, led by many different bands, proud of their impressive history which began during the Middle Ages as an unpaid voluntary arrangement to protect people and property during times of wars, pestilence and religious disputes.

It suited the town council and churches alike, lasting from the fourteenth century to the sixteenth century.

However, in the seventeenth century it was replaced by paid soldiers. The brotherhood lost their military duties and had to find new ways to continue. So, the Rifle Club Festival was born, concentrating mainly on entertaining their members with food, drink, music, dance and lots of other fun, a yearly highlight for young and old.

In later years sentimentality made Irmi cry whenever she watched their parade. But why? She became concerned how much music can be exploited, thinking especially about the time when Hitler's rifle men marched in full force to the same music to the same Market Square, showing off his power.

Thankfully perhaps there is one small consolation. Today's Rifle Club men only carry sports rifles, adorned with a flower. And still, Irmi's thoughts about what powerful role music has played throughout the centuries has made her cynical, in spite of her hope to waltz with Wonderful.

Is music a glorious Goddess or just a whore?

A pliant but dangerous servant to

power-politics, ideologies, religions and wars alike offering adaptable illusions

mirror-sounds of love, joy, ecstasy, sorrow, pain and solace

or the glory and fear of God

patriotism, torture, murder, death and bird song.

Chopin was *verboten* in the Warsaw Ghetto. However ironic, Jewish musicians were allowed to bring their instruments with them on the deportation-trains arriving on platform 2 of the freight depot.

Is music, that dubious commodity, a whoring Goddess?

20

Irmi is panicking. What if Wonderful comes to see her and expects more than she is prepared to give?

The words take her to a cliff. From there they want her to scream her fears into the wind because an old fairytale has come to haunt her imagination again.

She begs the words to understand, be patient with her as her thoughts take over, quietly at first.

Enjoy watching her, always have. How beautiful she is! Her golden heart dances through the high grass, kissing weeds and wild poppies. She runs after it, laughing. Stops by a moss-covered well, throwing her heart high up to the sun, happy.

Oh dear, oh dear, it has fallen into the well. What now? Sobbing, sobbing, sobbing...

Now Irmi's screaming starts:

"I knew it. There he is that fat, ugly frog, well practised in preying on women in distress. Stroking her hand now, whispering, promising to fetch her heart from the well if ... Of course, she kisses him. Another fool, blind, always grateful, hoping that her frog will always be kind, helpful and turn into a prince one day so that they can live happily ever after."

For a long time now Irmi has believed she knows better. Her screams are competing with a strong gust of wind from the sea now.

"Yes, love can strike unexpectedly. I accept that. But what if it turns out to be a dung-heap? What do you do then?"

She thinks she has all the answers. Her thoughts are racing.

Sit happily on top with a false smile, ignoring the stench, all in the name of love?

Or, de-dung the heap and rescue what can still be used as a fertiliser on your flowerbed of compromises?

Or, spray the dung with expensive perfume and plant red roses all around it to gloss over the lingering smell of disappointment.

Or even worse, hold on tightly to your dream of love, stubborn as a mule, protesting to the world. This dung is mine. I love it. Don't you dare burst my bubble!

Until you start to stink yourself.

Irmi is really screaming now.

"Can you hear me? Forget it girls! Not that anyone is going to listen to me. Understandably so! This powerful game has been protected throughout the centuries. Still, here is my new motto:

Love me, or stuff me with gooseberries, but listen mate, I have decided to play my love-tune on my very own, special bagpipes from now on. Okay? LONG LIVE THE PURSUIT OF HAPPINESS!"

Has she convinced the words? They listened patiently as always to her fears. They love her and want to protect her, asking her to go down to the beach and sit on her favourite boulder. It should calm her down, hopefully.

The sun is coming through. The sea licks at a tuft of grass, embroidered with pinhead purple petals securely anchored to a wet rock.

The flowers are determined, proud, with straight stalks, imitating the spiky grass in the sand, not greedy like the sea, licking, licking, licking, forever moving closer. Instead they are fearless and modestly glorious, just for today.

The water is see-through, patches of blue and dark green at the bottom, white too. Ragged bits, stringy, plum-purple drag along until pushed onto tired rocks. Teasing waves belittle their slippery struggle to float freely again.

Irmi goes down to sit on the sand. It is warm. She sees a drop of light fall onto her boulder. Philosopher's gold from mystery's throne. She strokes what can be touched. It whispers softly in return shy, dust-veiled secrets.

Then, Irmi cannot believe it. There it is, in the distance, his boat. She jumps up, waving and shouting:

"Wonderful, Wonderful!"

Forgotten are her fears. She simply wants to see him again. He has spotted her too, waving back. When he gets off the boat both run towards each other and embrace, quite naturally.

"What a wonderful surprise, my Wonderful!"

"And how is my Fury?"

Both are laughing.

"What a day! Let's take this lot in first and then sit in the sunshine! I've brought a picnic. You always spoiled me. It's my turn today."

It doesn't take long and the two of them sit close to the sea on an old blanket, ready for the picnic food.

"It's lovely to see you again."

Surprising herself, Irmi does mean it.

"I know, people do miss me, you know." He touches her hand.

"And how was New York? Thanks for the postcard."

"Hectic, hectic, hectic. Big cities are not for me. Not for too long, that is. But I saw my relatives which was nice. They are all well."

"Glad to hear it. And you?"

"Have been looking forward to our talks. What about you?"

"Me too, but where do we start?"

"Remember when I told you that my aunt took me to America when I was a boy to get a broader education there? But the main reason was that we were in danger."

"What kind of danger?"

"As I got older she explained it to me."

He stops for a while, stroking her hand.

"My aunt always loved films, you see. During the Weimar Republic the German film industry had a world-wide reputation for originality and creativeness, but it was Hitler's view that those films were too full of Jewish and liberal influences. He wanted to remove all that and clothe films in his National Socialist ideology instead."

"That is completely new to me. Go on!"

"He found the right man for this, Goebbels, who became the Minister for Public Enlightenment and Propaganda, who relished the prospect of controlling the film industry because he was not just interested in films, he was obsessed by them. Now he could indulge his favourite pastime."

"How clever!"

"Very. To win public support he started to produce feature films which offered escapism."

"Escapism? I do know only too well how that works."

"The films were popular for a while but by 1937 the German film industry was nationalised and in 1939 began a series of anti-Semitic films."

"Have you ever seen one?"

"No, but my aunt saw one of the worst films of this kind *JUD SÜSS*. She knew then that it was time for us to leave Germany."

Irmi is moving closer to him, touching his hair. Her thoughts racing.

"You can guess what I am going to say, can't you? Here it comes. I am your wonderful Jew Jacob Weiss."

Irmi just looks at him. Did he really say that? Then she smiles and ruffles his hair.

"Jacob, the Wonderful. Why didn't you tell me before?"

"Sorry, that's me. I knew how much you were struggling with what happened to us Jews, wanting desperately to know why, feeling guilty. You, always so full of fury for our plight."

Irmi touches his face. "Did you see that film?"

"No. I believe it is only shown in educational establishments now, always under supervision, in schools, colleges, universities etc. to explain to the students of today how low the Nazis and Goebbels stooped in their hatred for us Jews."

"Do you think we need to see it, Jacob?"

She likes using his real name. He can tell and is pleased.

"Not sure. Don't really want to. My aunt also told me how difficult it was for Jewish actors. One went as far as dying his hair and beard blonde, specialising in Aryan roles, much praised by the Nazis. He later revealed who he really was and escaped to Hollywood."

"Unbelievable, Jacob! I am so glad we were just children at that time. It must have been absolutely terrifying for your relatives."

"Well, it definitely was for another young actor who had married a Jewish woman. He was ordered to divorce his wife and leave his half-Jewish child."

"Cruel pigs!"

"Then in 1940 the Gestapo accused his wife of race-defilement and ordered her to pack her bags to join the Jewish Deportation. Finally, the Gestapo raided their home and found all three of them dead. The news spread quickly through Berlin's Artistic Quarter. There was a revolt in the film studios, my aunt said."

"Good for them! Isn't it outrageous what that bastard got away with? Jacob, will we ever really understand, especially you. Why all that hatred for the Jews? I doubt it."

"Me too, but at least British and American bombing raids crippled the Nazi film industry during the latter part of the war."

"Oh Jacob, I am so glad you were safe in America. But what about your father after your mother's death. Did he join you?"

Jacob is walking up and down. He does not want to tell her and yet he knows that he has to.

"My father was taken to a concentration camp in Auschwitz."

Irmi has joined him walking up and down. Tears are running down her face.

"Oh Jacob, no, no, no! Not your dear father too."

They embrace. Both are crying. Suddenly, Irmi's fury takes over. She runs fully clothed into the sea screaming obscenities. He runs after her trying to calm her down.

"He is fine now, my love. It is not your fault. It never was."

She keeps on swearing. There they are, holding on to each other, ignoring the incoming tidal waves. It has started to rain.

"How can you be so reasonable about it, Jacob? Why don't you scream against the heavens?"

"I do have my moments, you know, but my father is alive and we are here to make sure such hatred never gets out of control again anywhere, in whatever form."

Irmi tries to control her fury for Jacob's sake. She is shivering.

"We have to take these wet clothes off. Come on!"

They walk back to the house hand in hand. Irmi changes into her kaftan and finds old working clothes for Jacob. Both are quiet now but the pain shows in their faces.

After a while Irmi breaks the silence.

"We got on really well your dad and I while you were away. He is such a lovely man. How did he survive that hell?"

"He does not talk about it, not really. My aunt and I came back to look after him when it was all over. He was very thin and could hardly walk. It took a long time for him to recover."

"What about bitterness and anger?"

"I asked him once. He said: *When you have been where I have been and seen what I have seen, you know that there is no longer room for bitterness or anger in your heart, it does not help, only a deep and lonely sadness and grief for those who died as they did.*"

"What a wise and generous man your dear dad is! And here I am screaming, wanting answers, feeling sorry for myself. I am so ashamed now. What do I know about suffering? Nothing at all."

"Come, let us sit together and listen to a wonderful record I brought for you from New York to calm our pain for Dad and all those innocent people who suffered and died because of one man's murderous madness."

Summertime and the living is easy...

As the music and words touch their hearts, both are wishing that somehow the song will bring hope for their summer, helping Jacob's dad and them with their pain.

21

Listening quietly to the music helped both of them.

"What a lovely song it is, Jacob! Thank you for bringing it. Let it be our song from now on."

"It is special, Gershwin, you know. I believe it helped groups of people with deep grievances all over the world like the black Americans for example who all adopted it as their song of hope."

"Marvellous, how powerful music and words can be!"

"I would very much like to hear about you now."

"Are you sure?"

"Only if you want to tell me."

"Well, here it comes. I never belonged anywhere, not really, but I have two wonderful aunts Sarah and Toba, my mother Yetta's sisters. They brought me up together with Farmer Moller on his farm where they worked before and after the war, doing their very best to give me a happy childhood. I will always be grateful to them."

"But what about your parents?"

"My mother didn't want me. She gave me away, a baby, for her sisters to look after."

"Why?"

"Don't know. Not important any more. It's over."

"Are you sure?"

"My aunts refused to tell me the real reason, just made up excuses for my mother, illness, that sort of thing, not to hurt me even more because I was so very jealous of my brother Klaus. Mother adored him."

"And your father?"

"He tried to make up for it, spoiled me. He loved me. I know he did, but he had to choose, didn't he? Mother or me for whatever reason."

Jacob is uneasy.

"How painful that must have been for you as a child."

"It was, but the love my aunts and Farmer Moller gave me helped. Later, as an adult, empty pretence communications between my parents and me nearly killed me. That is why my contact with them ended altogether one year."

"Where are your aunts now?"

"Still in Susato. Sarah married Farmer Moller's nephew Otto, a wounded soldier who came to live on the farm to recover during the war. One of his legs had to be amputated. Aunt Sarah was his nurse. They deserve to be happy. They are. I know they are."

"Do you still keep in contact with them?"

"Not really. Didn't want to be in the way. Told them I needed time to myself, sort myself out, that sort of thing. Wait, I'll show you their wedding photo."

It does not take long for her to find the photo.

"Interesting. Is that you, the little girl in the middle?"

"It is. Aunts Toba and Ruth on the right with husband Horst. Mother and father on the left and Farmer Moller, the tall man, at the back."

"I'll bring photos of my relatives in America next time."

"Don't forget!"

"Do any of your relatives know where you are?"

"No. Don't want them to know."

Jacob feels more and more sorry for his Fury but does not want to show it. Maybe sharing it all with him might help her.

"What happened to them all after the war?"

"Aunt Toba, the youngest sister, is a gifted seamstress. She never married. Opened her own business after the war in Susato. Very successful too. I used to help her as a teenager. Enjoyed it for a while but wasn't very good at it. Look!"

She shows him a big hole in her kaftan which could have done with a stitch or two.

"And your aunt Ruth and her husband Horst?"

Irmi does not answer right away. Jacob senses that there is something. Patience!

"Horst got involved with the Nazis. Looked after the Hitler Youth in Susato, enthusiastically that is, believing that it was a good thing for the children. Was later a soldier in Hitler's war, ending up in Russia as a prisoner of war for a long time. A broken man when he came home. I felt sorry for him. I always liked him."

Jacob can see how uncomfortable she is talking about him. Maybe some other time. It has been a long, emotional day. They decide to go for a walk. The sun doesn't let them down, forcing its way through the mist.

Suddenly Jacob stops, lets go of Irmi's hand.

"Just by the way, sweetie. What is your name ?"

"Didn't know you could be sarcastic. I like Fury. Not sure whether to tell you."

They sit under a tree. Irmi has brought two apples.

"I am waiting."

"All right then." Irmi pauses. "It's Irmi Lange. You can call me Irmilein. My aunts and Farmer Moller always did."

"Irmilein, my Irmilein. I like it."

"I have another present for you. Are you ready?"

"Always."

They have eaten their apples. Irmi looks really happy.

"Jacob, my grandma Brana was Jewish like you. What about that?"

"Never! How come?"

"She came from Poland as a young girl, all alone and worked for Farmer Moller. Never told anybody about herself. Married a Catholic and had four daughters. Granddad died tragically. I never met him. I'll tell you about all that some other time."

"Did your grandma survive?"

"Nobody knew that she was Jewish. She kept it very quiet right from the beginning. It never occurred to the rest of the family until she told them one day, aware of the danger for all of them from Hitler's plans. As far as they knew they were just an ordinary Catholic family."

"You know, if your grandma is Jewish you are too?"

"So people told me. It follows they said, from grandmother to mother to daughter to granddaughter. I never considered it, not really. Maybe I am. All I am conscious of is that I am ashamed to be German."

"But I am German too."

Irmi is not prepared to reply to that now. There will be plenty of time to look at it another day. Of course he is German. What else would he be? Many people refuse to consider that, even today. To them he is just that Jew.

"And where was your grandma during the Hitler Years?"

"I have another very special grandma Elizabeth and aunt Erna, my dad's mother and sister. They were real heroes, hiding and protecting Brana in their attic."

"Is she still alive now?"

"She died two years ago. Farmer Moller took her in after her lonely ordeal hidden away in the attic for so long. She worked for him as before but became his wife later. Nobody was surprised. He had always loved her, secretly that is. He insisted on a Jewish wedding ceremony. Wasn't that a lovely thought after all she had been through? It was all very secret, just the two of them somewhere. His wedding present was a wonderful surprise for her. He built her *a Succah* in the garden. I can still picture this little wooden hut, its roof made of branches and leaves and most importantly with sufficient spaces between to see the stars. We, the children, decorated it with lots of fruit hanging from the roof."

"That sounds fantastic. We never had one."

"Grandma told us about Poland when she was a child. How lovely it always was at harvest time and how her family even ate all their meals in it throughout the seven days of the *Succot,* the Festival of Tabernacles. And there it was for all of us to enjoy. We had lots of fun.

"When she died she was buried in the Jewish Cemetery in Susato. Farmer Moller only lived another six months after her death and wanted to be buried next to her. I do miss them."

"Now, that is something! Susato's Romeo and Juliet."

"Farmer Moller left me some money in his will. That is why I can be independent now, just writing."

"Writing your bestseller?"

"Something worthwhile, I hope, says your arrogant Irmi."

"I am exhausted. What about you?"

"Just one more thing, Jacob, my Jacob. Let's do something very special for your dad. Let's build him *a Succah* during the summer, ready for harvest time. What do you think?"

Jacob is crying, but smiling.

"What a wonderful girl you are! A great idea! We'll start soon. I'll bring all the tools we might need."

"Hope you are handy because I am not!"

Jacob smiles.

"Will you be all right if I leave you now? Father needs help in the shop. He is not getting any younger."

"I'll be fine. I am so glad we talked, however sad at times."

Two loners walk hand in hand to his boat, hopefully at the beginning of a true relationship.

22

Jacob and Irmi have started to build the *Succah.* They really enjoy it. There is plenty of wood on the island. Old trees have been blown over by the strong winter storms.

Their summer has been glorious. Besides carrying heavy branches and trying to fit it all together they also relax and talk. Jacob stays whole days now encouraged by his father.

"I am fine and I will find someone to help me in the shop. You make the best of the sunshine. I still remember enjoying wonderful days with family and friends there. A shame you had to be in America as a boy, missing out on all that. Enjoy our island now with your friend. I like her."

Jacob does and finally finds the courage to tell Irmi an important secret about himself, hoping that it will not spoil things. They are lying on the beach relaxing after a long swim.

Irmi is like a fish, he thinks.

"I really like the look of our *Succah,* Jacob. We have done well, haven't we, never building anything before."

"Father will love it, I know he will."

"Go on, what is it? You have been wanting to tell me all day."

"How did you know?"

"Just do."

"Well Irmi... I am a painter. It would be fantastic if I could come and paint here like my father's granddad. You never know, I might become famous like he was."

" Of course you will, big-head!"

"I promise not to intrude on your privacy. Need to be alone just like you, always have. The boat has been my escape from the world so far."

98

Irmi looks worried. He is waiting patiently for her reply. At last...

"Don't see why not. Could try it for a while. We have got on with one another so far, haven't we?"

"Irmilein, my beautiful Irmilein!"

"Don't go overboard, sailor! Come on, let's have another swim!"

The summer is slowly turning into autumn, harvest time. The *Succah* is ready and looks very similar to Grandma Brana's in Farmer Moller's garden in Susato. Inside are a table and three old chairs. It is time to invite Jacob's father.

"What are you going to tell him tomorrow?"

"I'll think of something. We've got the new help in the shop now anyway. More time to spend here."

"I am really looking forward to it. Plenty of time to do some baking this evening. Get it ready early on. Bring some fruit with you. We'll let your dad fasten it to the roof."

Next day Irmi is sitting on her boulder, all excited, wondering when they might be arriving. Hurray, there they come! Jacob helps his father off the boat.

"Hello my dear. You are looking healthy, nice and brown."

"Her name is Irmi, Dad."

"So happy to see you again, Mr Weiss. Are you well?"

"Couldn't be better. Jacob said you two have a surprise for me."

"We have. We hope you'll like it."

"Come on, Dad!"

They walk very slowly along the sandy path. Halfway they stop.

"Close your eyes now, Dad! We are nearly there."

Jacob takes his father's arm.

"Open now!"

And there it is, their *Succah*. The father is speechless. He pretends not to cry, laughs instead.

"What a surprise, you two! It has been a long time since I saw one."

They go inside. The table is set, coffee in a flask.

"I don't believe it, my dear. I tasted most of your cakes already, remember, but *these ... Potato Latkes, Hamentaschen* and *Matzomeal Sponge Cake.* How did you know about all that?"

"My grandma used to make them for us children."

"Your mother did the very same, Jacob. Well, let's celebrate the Feast of Tabernacles together. Thank you so much, you two."

They spent the afternoon inside the *Succah* enjoying food and drink. Fruit is hanging from the roof now. Jacob's father had fun putting it there. When it is getting darker he takes his son's hand.

"Let's visit your mother now. She has to be part of this happy day."

Irmi doesn't understand.

In the evening mist they follow the narrow path to the place of their longing, pushing aside low, defenceless branches and stumble over exposed willow roots. Thistles and nettles shiver in the breeze, no longer defending their territory. Lost, silver streaks dart through tired trees as darkness sneaks in slowly. Surprisingly for Irmi they arrive at those three graves she visited and wondered about before.

"Dad, Irmi doesn't know. I haven't told her."

"My dear, here rest my grandfather the famous painter, my father and my wife Rachel."

Silently Irmi joins them in touching the gravestones. As they touch them, whispering to their loved ones, the stones warm to their hands. On their way back plump, bored raindrops slide slowly from careless leaves.

"Time to go home now. How can I ever thank you two for such a unique surprise?"

Irmi is lying on her bed. She cannot sleep. What a wonderful day it has been! Suddenly she hears Jacob's voice.

"Come out, Irmilein!"

He has returned in the middle of the night.

"Coming."

The Succah

He puts his arm around her shoulders and they walk into the night to the *Succah.*

"I simply had to come back to look at the stars with you."

They are counting how many stars they can see through the branches of the roof until they fall asleep in each other's arms.

Will the icy light of a silver moon break through
the clouds as a flower grows silently,
unfolding its golden leaves?

The air is still, yet full of anguish
as the night yearns for light,
waiting for love in its splendour
to come down on a moonbeam, blue,
breathing mystery, cooling a stream of doubt.

Don't touch the flower!
Let it grow in silence,
revealing its loving loneliness.

EPILOGUE

Peace, please!

Stolpersteine

Was it just a warning, or his very personal demand for peace and reconciliation that prompted the Cologne artist ***Gunter Demning*** to create those 'Stolpersteine' (stumbling blocks)?

They are small cobblestone-sized concrete cube 4 inches square, covered with a sheet of brass, a memorial for individual victims of Nazism. The vast majority commemorate Jewish victims of the Holocaust.

Many of these stones now lie flush with the pavement or sidewalk in front of the last residence of the victim. Most stones have similar inscriptions:

Here resided

Name

Date of Birth

Year of Deportation

Concentration Camp

Murdered/missing

The information comes from schools, surviving relatives and

103

various organizations, especially from the database of the Yad Yashem in Jerusalem.

At first the artist had doubts whether it would be possible to activate his memorial plan because there were so many victims to be considered. But a Cologne priest of the Antoniter church encouraged his idea.

Since then there are over 7500 Stolpersteine in more than 90 German towns and cities, financed and supported by generous donations and town councils.

The list of places that have these memorials now extends to several countries.

An important, main critique about Demning's project comes from Charlotte Knobloch, the once president of the Central Jewish Committee in Germany. She thought it unbearable for people to trample over stones with the names of murdered Jews. Of course this is a worthy, heartfelt response. Many Jews are bound to agree, but others defend Demnig's intentions. The victims in the concentration camps were degraded to just numbers. He wanted to give them their names back so that the person would never be forgotten. He even saw the necessity to bend down to read what was written on the stone as a symbolic bowing to these victims.

Will the Stolpersteine as a warning be helpful in the demand for world peace, especially now, when again more and more wars cause ordinary people to suffer the consequences of power struggles, wrong decisions by politicians, even madness?

How many of us work towards a contribution for world peace, however small?

Maybe someone will come up with a new idea to make the world live in peace with patience and understanding for each others ways and respect for life, so that we do not need memorial stones in the future.

ACKNOWLEDGEMENTS

A special thank you goes to my always patient and most helpful editor at **SCRIPTORA,** also to **Alfred Gewohn** for his Cover Design, **Tony Murray** for Graphics and **Linda Goulden** for Images.

And to the **Füllhorn, a Soest Magazine** which accepted many of my articles, poems and short stories.

Forever grateful to the **Inklings,** a **Liverpool Writers Group** for their patient support throughout the years.

OTHER PUBLICATIONS BY ALFA

WORD WATCHING (Poems in English)
SPIEGELSPLITTER (Poems in German)
CHAOS (Poems and Short Stories in English and German)
SUSATO (German Version)

AMATEUR GRAMMATICS
Four booklets for students of the German language, suitable for beginners and advanced study.

BROADCASTS
Radio Merseyside and Radio Cumbria

MAIN PRIZES
Julia Cairns Salver twice (1989 & 2003)
from the **Society of Women Writers and Journalists**
Bard of the Year 1994
100 Best Poets - Forward Press
Southport Seminar (Monologue)
Miners' Eisteddfford - South Wales (Poems & Short Stories)
Dun Laoghaire- Rathdown - Ireland (Poems in German)

Also widely published in literary magazines and anthologies (Poems and Prose).

Distribution of all books – Erika Goulden
Email: erika.goulden@o2.co.uk
Websites: www.alfa-erikagoulden.com
www.swwj.info
Direct Line: 0151 734 1341
Overseas line: 0044 151 734 1341